AMISH HARVEST TIME

BOOK 38 THE AMISH BONNET SISTERS

SAMANTHA PRICE

CHAPTER 1

The first rays of dawn gently touched the horizon as Wilma Baker stepped outside her home. The front door creaked, prompting her to swing it open and shut a few times, reminding herself to oil the hinges later. She was determined to become more self-reliant, even though she had plenty of people willing to help.

Wilma wouldn't be perceived as one of those help-less women incapable of doing anything. Of course, she wouldn't refuse assistance when it came to chopping wood; that was a task she happily left to others.

Throughout the previous night, she couldn't shake her thoughts about Obadiah, replaying the decision to let him go over and over in her mind. Decision-making had always been a struggle, and she often found it easier when others made choices for her. This time, she had to trust her judgment.

Wilma inhaled deeply of the sweet aroma of ripening apples. The harvest season was drawing near, and the orchard's fragrance was a reminder of the fruitful days to come. It was a time when the air seemed to carry the promise of new beginnings.

"Ah, another splendid day," she whispered, a smile tugging at the corners of her lips. Glancing over, she noticed her porch was empty, making it all the more perfect. Ignoring Matthew must have done the trick, or perhaps he had already moved on from Krystal. Nevertheless, a heap of his belongings remained scattered on the porch, a silent reminder of his presence. She hoped he would soon return to retrieve them.

Red, her faithful companion, pushed his way out the door and stood by her side. With everyone still asleep, she seized the opportunity for a brisk walk. As they strolled down the rows of trees, Red kept pace with her, his loyal presence providing comfort.

"Good boy," she said, patting his head affectionately. There was something about Red that she couldn't fully explain. Somehow, he seemed to understand her, and in return, she felt an inexplicable connection with the gentle creature. He, too, was searching for his place in the world, just as she was finding her own.

The breeze gently swayed the tree branches, causing the laden fruit to sway like pendulums. Each apple served as a testament to the love and care poured into the orchard over the years.

"Ah, Josiah," she murmured softly, her fingers gently

tracing the initials she had carved long ago into the weathered trunk of an old tree. "You were taken away too soon. Too soon for me, anyway." She looked up at the vast expanse of the sky above. "Lord, I know You have Your reasons for taking Josiah and then Levi from me, but sometimes... sometimes it's hard to live with this emptiness."

Wilma steadied herself, wiping away her tears with the edge of her apron. She knew it was far less painful if she didn't dwell on the memories of her late husbands. But how could she not think about Josiah when she walked through the trees? This was his place, and something of him seemed to linger among the trees he had planted. The orchard still bore his name, a testament to his labor and love. And as for Levi, the orchard held countless memories of him as well.

Looking out at all the apples, she was pleased for the upcoming harvest. Fairfax had worked tirelessly, and Florence had made the right choice in appointing him as the manager.

Wilma reached up and plucked an apple from the tree, holding it up to the morning light. Its rosy skin reflected the golden rays, casting a warm glow over her face. "I'll need someone to start making cider. And I'll make apple pies for the shop. Maybe even try a new recipe for jelly," she mused aloud. She turned to Red, who was sitting nearby with his soulful brown eyes fixed on her.

"What do you think, Red?" she asked with a smile, though she knew he couldn't respond with words.

Red merely blinked, understanding in his own way.

Wilma fashioned a makeshift pouch by looping up her apron and began moving from tree to tree, her hands expertly plucking apples and gently placing them into her apron. The rhythm of the orchard and the rustling leaves enveloped her, bringing a sense of peace and purpose.

This was where she belonged — amidst the whispering leaves and the sweet scent of ripening fruit. It was in the orchard that she found solace and strength, cherishing the memories of her beloved husbands and embracing the hope for a bountiful future.

CHAPTER 2

*F*avor leaned against the porch railing, one hand resting on her still-flat stomach. She breathed the morning air deeply.

"Feeling better today, Favor?" Simon called from the yard where he stood with his father, Melvin, and their neighbor, Zeke. They were discussing the details of their new alpaca farm venture.

"I am," she replied, smiling at her husband. "Much better, thank you." She took another deep breath, enjoying one day free of morning sickness.

She grimaced when she thought about when Harriet and Melvin moved to their temporary home. She'd been feeling so helpless she'd nearly asked Harriet to move in permanently.

It was a low moment that might have changed her future. That would've been awful because Simon and she would never have been alone.

"Good," Simon replied, grinning back at her. He turned to his father and went back to discussing the best way to construct the alpaca enclosures.

Melvin looked over at Favor. "Are you sure you don't want to come over here and help us plan, Favor? You always have such creative ideas."

Favor laughed. "I'm not sure that is true, but I can't. Ma has given me orders to rest."

"Ah, yes," Melvin chuckled, nodding in agreement. "We better not cross Ma."

Favor smiled at her father-in-law. It was nice to feel included. She and Simon still hadn't shared their pregnancy news with anyone. Harriet would fuss even more if she knew that.

When a thought occurred to Favor, she waited until the men had finished their conversation. "Simon, what if we get Ma to paint a mural on the side of the barn? It could be something bright and cheerful to welcome the alpacas to their new home."

Simon looked thoughtful for a moment, rubbing his chin. Then he grinned. "That's a wonderful idea. You and Ma can put your heads together and come up with a design. As long as it's not too bright. We don't want to scare the alpacas."

"Okay," she replied, loving the excitement of a new project. She watched as the men continued to discuss their plans, her thoughts drifting to the future – to the baby growing inside her and the love that would bind them all together.

Harriet burst through the door with the empty washing basket wedged on her hip. She set it down, staring at Favor. "There you are. Why are you on your feet?"

"I was just seeing what they're doing out there." When Harriet continued to glare at Favor, she moved inside to the couch. Harriet followed her picking up a blanket and throwing it over her legs.

"Stay there and I'll bring your breakfast."

"Thanks, Ma, but I'm not that hungry."

"Just eat what you can." Harriet disappeared and returned with a tray.

Favor had expected a cooked breakfast of bacon and eggs, but instead, there was plain buttered toast and a cup of black coffee. "Thank you."

Harriet settled herself into a chair and picked up the delicate needlework she had brought with her. "Now, I heard someone say something about a mural," she said, curiosity sparkling in her eyes.

Favor took a sip of her coffee, contemplating the idea. "I was just thinking about a mural on the barn. Would you like to do that? You're good at painting, like the flowers you painted in the kitchen."

Harriet raised an eyebrow playfully. "You want flowers on the barn?"

Favor giggled, shaking her head. "No, something else. Something suitable. Will you do it?"

A warm smile spread across Harriet's face. "I'd love that."

"Simon said for us to work on a design together," Favor added.

"Alright, but I'll be the only one climbing a ladder. You must rest in your condition," Harriet said, concern lacing her words as she shifted her gaze to her needlework.

Favor's eyes widened, her heart pounding in her chest as she realized her mother-in-law knew. "Ma, you know?" she asked softly.

Harriet blinked rapidly, her eyes meeting Favors with a mix of surprise and joy. "It's true?" she whispered.

Favor nodded, a radiant smile lighting up her face. "Yes."

Overcome with emotion, Harriet rushed to hug her, letting her needlework fall to the floor. Favor laughed warmly, carefully holding her coffee away from the embrace. "Careful of the coffee."

Harriet pulled back, her eyes glistening with tears. "Oh, Favor, I'm so happy for you. For both of you," she said, her voice filled with genuine happiness.

Favor's heart swelled with gratitude for her mother-in-law's support. "Thank you, Ma. Your blessings mean the world to me."

Harriet beamed. "And when the little one arrives, you'll see, I'll be even more helpful."

Favor nodded, touched by Harriet's warmth. "I know you will, Ma. You've always been there for us, and I couldn't ask for a better mother-in-law."

Harriet took the coffee from her and set it down on the table, and then gave Favor a giant hug, nearly pushing all the air out of her. Harriet then jumped back and Favor couldn't help laughing at her.

"How did you know? Don't tell me Simon told you. I'll be so mad at him."

"No. He didn't, but he should've. Why did you both keep it from me?" Harriet scooted her over and sat on the couch with her.

"It's only early days. I just want to make sure we get further along before we tell anyone."

"I couldn't be happier."

"Did you tell Melvin you thought I might be pregnant?" Favor asked.

Harriet shook her head. "No. I wasn't totally sure. I didn't want to tell him my suspicions in case I was wrong. I'm glad I was right."

"Are you sure you understand why we didn't tell you right away?"

Harriet held Favor's hand. "I understand, dear. You both wanted to be sure. But remember, Melvin and I are here for both of you, no matter what. You can lean on us."

"Thank you, Ma. That means a lot to us."

They shared a warm smile. Just then, Harriet's eyes went wide as she realized something. "Oh, dear! You're going to be showing soon. We need to start sewing you bigger dresses!"

Favor looked down at her tummy, trying to imagine what it would feel like to get bigger. "I guess we do."

Just then, Simon, Melvin, and Zeke walked inside, their faces flushed from the cold morning air. Melvin asked, "What's so funny, ladies?"

Harriet winked at Favor. "Just planning some future projects. Right, Favor?"

Favor nodded, her cheeks pink, but not from the chill. "That's right, Pa. Future projects."

Simon looked at her with a twinkle in his eye. "Well, as long as these future projects don't interfere with the mural."

"We'll come up with something spectacular," Harriet said.

Melvin drew his eyebrows together. "Don't make it too bright. We don't want to be the talk of the town."

"It'll be just right." Harriet and Favor exchanged amused glances, their shared secret adding a layer of warmth to the cold morning.

Zeke and Melvin went into the kitchen and Simon bent down to kiss Favor's forehead before heading inside to wash up.

"Favor, dear, we should start on the design after you finish breakfast. What do you say?"

Favor looked at Harriet. "Yes, let's do that. And, thank you, Ma."

"For what, dear?"

"For everything," Favor replied, her voice brimming with emotion. "For being here."

Harriet beamed at her. "Well, dear, that's why I'm here, to be here."

Favor leaned closer and whispered, "When should we tell Melvin? It doesn't seem fair that we all know and he doesn't."

Harriet paused for a moment, considering the question. "We should probably tell him soon. He's a bit more observant than you think, and he'll be wondering what's going on with all the secret conversations and whispers."

Favor nodded. "You're right. It's just that I'm a little nervous about telling him so soon. What if something unthinkable happens?"

Harriet gave her hand a comforting squeeze. "Don't worry, dear. I'm sure you will have a healthy baby. I know it. I've been praying for this for a long time. Have faith."

Favor smiled, feeling reassured. "Okay, Ma. We'll tell him soon, but it's still too early to tell anyone else. Don't you agree?"

Harriet nodded.

After breakfast, they worked on the design for the mural, their heads bent together in concentration as they sketched out ideas and discussed color schemes.

CHAPTER 3

*A*fter breakfast when Wilma was alone, she headed down to the small shop on her property.

She inserted the key and pushed the door open.

Dust-covered countertops and empty shelves greeted her.

A nostalgic smile played on her lips as she stepped further inside, feeling the warmth of sunlight cascading through the window onto the well-worn wooden floors. The memories of her girls busily arranging the apple products flooded her mind. She could almost hear their laughter.

A sense of purpose filled Wilma's heart as she began to tidy the shop. With each stroke of the rag along the countertop, the layers of dust vanished, revealing the weathered surface beneath.

A gentle breeze swept through the door, carrying a hint of fresh air and possibility.

Her peace was short-lived because Ada came bustling through the doorway with a pot of tea in her hands.

Wilma burst out laughing. "Oh, Ada, you brought tea from your place? You know I have tea."

"I want you to taste this particular tea. It's Debbie's tea. It's the first time I tried it. Have you tasted her apple blossom tea?"

Wilma thought for a moment. She couldn't keep up with all the new tea varieties Debbie was coming up with. "I don't think so."

Ada put the teapot down, and Wilma found some cups in the cupboard and poured herself some tea.

Wilma tasted it and agreed that it was good. "Debbie will want to sell her tea here."

"I know, and we can offer samples. We'll borrow Matthew's tiny gas heater to boil water." Ada chuckled.

Wilma nodded. "I like the idea. He's still got his things on the porch."

"If you like that, I have another idea."

Wilma braced herself to hear it. "Go on."

"We talked before about doing more for charity this year. The year's more than half over. I said we could combine this store with charity work."

"Yes? So, what's your idea?"

Ada grinned. "I was up all night thinking about this.

Wait for it... An apple pie contest. I think it would be a fun way to raise money."

"An apple pie contest?" Wilma echoed, her eyes lighting up at the thought. "You mean people bake apple pies and put them in a contest?"

"Yes, exactly that. Well, what do you think?"

Wilma's face lit up. "I love it. That sounds delightful. And you know I make the best apple pies in the county." She winked playfully at Ada. "I'll win by a mile."

"Sadly, you probably would, but since I'll be entering a pie, you'll come second." Ada chuckled. "We just need to find three judges to keep things fair."

Wilma leaned against the doorframe, deep in thought. "Well, let's see... How about we ask Maddie from the bakery? She certainly knows a good pie when she tastes one."

Ada nodded. "Good choice. What about Esther from the quilting circle? She always has strong opinions on everything."

"Ah, yes," Wilma said, remembering Esther's harsh critiques. She didn't even show her the quilt they made for Cherish for fear of disapproval. She would've been upset by the non-traditional use of appliqué. "Then we need one more judge."

"Susan and Daphne can help."

"They'd love that, I'm sure. They'll be here soon."

Wilma was pleased to have another distraction besides reopening the store. It would stop her from thinking about Obadiah.

"You've got that faraway look in your eyes again."

Wilma looked over at her best friend. She'd never been able to keep secrets from her. Well, she had never told her about the kiss she'd shared with Obadiah, and neither would she share it with anyone.

"Thinking about him again?" Ada inquired when Wilma was slow to speak.

Wilma nodded. "I just don't know whether I made the right choice. He wanted more and I told him I couldn't have another marriage."

"What are you worried about? You made your choice."

Wilma bit her lip. "I just don't know if it was the right choice."

"I wasn't sure if things had gone that far, but I thought they might have." Ada puffed out her cheeks, looking down.

"Marriage was talked about. And I couldn't go through with losing someone again." Wilma hoped Ada wouldn't try to talk her into continuing things with Obadiah.

Ada nodded. "I was worried because we knew nothing about Obadiah's past. You might have known him as a youth, but there's a good missing fifty years that you know nothing about."

Wilma nodded.

Ada didn't wait for Wilma to reply. "You talked about choice. Perhaps there is no right or wrong. There is just a choice, and then you carry through with that decision. Although, Samuel will be disappointed. He got along very well with Obadiah."

Wilma raised her eyebrows. "I can't marry a man just to keep Samuel happy."

Ada chuckled. "I know, but he and Levi were such good friends and he misses him. It would've been good for him to have another close friend while you and I do things together."

Wilma considered Ada's words. She had made her choice, and now she had to live with the consequences. But that didn't ease the ache in her heart. She missed Obadiah and the feeling she had when she was with him. "I don't have any answers," Wilma said, her voice thick with emotion.

Ada placed a comforting hand on her shoulder. "I know, my dear. But you can't change the past. All you can do is move forward and leave everything in *Gott's* hands."

She took a deep breath and let it out slowly, feeling a sense of calm wash over her. "I think you're right," Wilma said, her voice steady. "Let's focus on the apple pie contest and raising money for charity. It's a good distraction."

Ada smiled. "If things between Obadiah and you are meant to be, they will be."

Wilma grinned, feeling a little brighter.

CHAPTER 4

That evening, as they gathered around the dinner table, Wilma glanced over at Jed and Krystal. They had a bright future ahead, and the way they looked at each other was simply heart-warming.

The delicious smell of stew filled the room, and Debbie had brought candles home from the markets and had set them on the table. The candlelight created dancing shadows on the walls.

"Guess what, everyone?" Jed's voice beamed with excitement, rising above the conversation. "I've got eight people booked for a tour on Friday!"

Ada and Samuel exchanged delighted glances while Wilma clapped her hands together in excitement.

"Jed, that's fantastic news!" Ada said, her eyes crinkling at the corners as she smiled warmly at him. "You and Krystal must be so pleased."

"We are. I couldn't have done it without you and

Samuel helping me." Jed's gaze traveled to the couple, and finally to Wilma, who beamed back at him like a proud mother hen.

Samuel smiled. "We're all praying for this to be a success."

"Did I ever tell you how fortunate I feel to have met all of you?" Jed asked. "I can't imagine my life without you all now. I never felt I belonged anywhere and then I met Krystal. Now I'm here, I know why she never wants to leave this community."

"We're all pleased you've come, Jed. You are one of the family now," Wilma replied, reaching across the table to pat his hand affectionately.

Debbie's curiosity finally got the better of her. "So, Jed," she began, leaning forward with a gleam in her eye, "where exactly are you taking these folks on your tour?"

Jed grinned and put down his knife and fork. "Well, before we head over to the orchard, I've arranged for us to visit Eddie's bees." He paused for effect, watching their expressions light up with interest. "Eddie is more than happy to show our guests the beehives and give a talk on how amazing bees are."

"Sounds fascinating," Ada commented.

"Absolutely," agreed Jed. "But that's not all. We're also going to stop by Krystal's quilt store. Krystal is going to talk to them about the quilts and what the various patterns represent. Then we'll visit an Amish bakery for lunch, the one that's run by one of our community members. Then we'll come to the orchard."

Ada waved a fork at him. "And don't forget to bring them to our little shop before they go. I'm sure they'd like to stock their larder with some of our offerings."

Everyone laughed at Ada.

"What's funny?" Ada asked.

Debbie shook her head. "It just sounded funny when you said larder. I don't think people use that word anymore."

"You won't think it's so funny if they buy your tea while they're there."

Debbie nodded. "No, I'll think that's good."

"That reminds me, we'll need more of your tea for our store, Debbie. I've got a nice spot for the tea boxes underneath the window."

"Thanks, Wilma."

Krystal still had the tours on her mind. "Don't you think the tour will be a great experience for the tourists?"

Samuel raised his eyebrows in approval. "Sounds like they'll have a good time."

"Yes, and of course, as we travel from one place to another, I'll be pointing out all the interesting sights along the way. I want to make sure they get a true taste of this beautiful place."

Wilma's eyes twinkled with delight. "I have no doubt that you'll give them the grandest tour they've ever experienced, Jed."

"Thank you, Wilma," Jed replied.

"Can I go on the tour too, Jed?" Jared piped up from the children's table, his big eyes wide with curiosity.

Jed glanced over at Debbie, seeking her guidance as he considered the boy's request. Debbie shook her head. "Sorry, Jared. You'll be in school on Friday."

"Aw, man!" Jared grumbled, stabbing his fork into a piece of meat. "I always miss out just because I'm a kid."

"Hey," Jed said, trying to lift his spirits. "There will be plenty more tours in the future. Maybe one day you can ride up front with me."

Jared's face lit up. "Could I, *Mamm?*"

"Maybe one day if it's not a school day."

Jared returned to eating his food. As Jed watched the child's excitement over something so simple as riding in a wagon, it reminded him of the fun he had growing up with his brothers. They got along great back then, but not so much now, though.

"By the way, Jed," Ada chimed in, drawing his attention back to the present moment. "You should talk to Daphne Hinkle. She not only knows all the history of the families in the community, she knows of all the town's stories."

Jed liked the sound of that. "Great idea, Ada. I could definitely use some urban legends or lesser-known facts to keep my guests entertained."

"Leave it to Daphne," Samuel agreed with a chuckle. "She's got enough stories to last you a lifetime."

"Perfect," Jed grinned. "I'll make sure to visit her before Friday."

"Isn't it funny, Jed," Ada mused, "that you're showing people around when you've only just arrived in town yourself?"

"Ah, well, what can I say? I'm a fast learner."

"And we're all so glad you've decided to settle in our little corner of the world, Jed," Debbie said.

"I might be new here, but I've fallen in love with this place. And when you love something, you want to share it with everyone."

"So when will you talk with Daphne?" Wilma asked.

"Maybe tomorrow. I'd love some of that local gossip to give the tourists."

"Gossip, huh?" Samuel chuckled, a sly smile playing at the corner of his lips. "Now that sounds like Ada's kind of tour!"

Ada playfully swatted Samuel's arm, suppressing a giggle. "Oh, you're just terrible! But seriously, Jed, Daphne is a wealth of knowledge. You won't be disappointed."

"Sounds great," Jed said. Yet, a small voice in the back of his mind whispered, would it be enough? Would the history and local color be sufficient to captivate his guests?

Samuel rubbed his beard. "The harvest is starting on Tuesday, and your tour is on Friday, correct?"

"That's right. Wilma told me the harvesting goes on

for weeks, so they don't need to be here on the very first day."

"I guess." Samuel nodded.

Jed stared at his older friend. "You seem doubtful, Samuel."

"No, I'm not. I just wondered if you knew what day was what."

"Thanks, Samuel. Is that what you think of me?"

Everyone laughed.

CHAPTER 5

*T*he following morning, Wilma Baker stood on her front porch, a basket of freshly picked tomatoes cradled in her arm. There were too many tomatoes to keep, and she was considering making relish out of them.

Red wagged his tail happily at her side.

She couldn't help but smile down at him, though she still questioned why she had allowed him into her life.

"Must be going soft in my old age," she murmured to herself. When she looked down the long driveway wondering when Ada would arrive, she saw a dusty pickup truck on the road.

She was surprised when it turned into her driveway. "Looks like we've got a visitor, Red."

The metal beast came to a halt near her porch, and a

tall, wiry man with unkempt hair and an unshaven face stepped out.

Immediately, Wilma felt uneasy. After all, she was totally alone.

"Mornin', ma'am," the man drawled as he approached Wilma. "Heard you got this here dog."

Wilma eyed him suspiciously, her grip on the basket tightening. There was something about the way he looked at Red that sent a shiver down her spine. "What's it to you?" she asked cautiously.

"Name's Cal. That there's my dog, ma'am." He extended a hand toward Red, who backed away and moved behind Wilma.

Wilma didn't shake his hand. "I'm not so sure he's your dog. He doesn't seem to like you much," she said.

"Ah, well, he's just bein' stubborn. Probably thinks he's found himself a new home." He lunged forward, grabbing Red by the scruff of his neck. The dog yelped as he hoisted him into the air.

"Stop!" Wilma cried out, dropping her basket of tomatoes. They tumbled to the ground scattering everywhere. "You're hurting him!"

"Mind your own business, woman. This is between me and my dog." With a sneer, the man carried Red to the bed of his pickup truck and threw him in. The dog whimpered, cowering in the corner.

"Please," Wilma begged, her heart aching for Red. "He doesn't want to go with you. How do I know he's your dog?"

"Like I said, mind your own business." He climbed into the driver's seat, the engine roaring to life. His gaze met hers one last time. "Don't go pokin' your nose where it don't belong."

And with that, he sped off, leaving a cloud of dust and despair in his wake.

Tears obscured Wilma's vision as she ran to hitch the horse and buggy. It was so hard being a woman alone. If that man had sensed there was a man around, he never would've acted the way that he had.

She climbed into her buggy. She whipped the reins, urging her horse onward to Ada's house, desperate for comfort and a plan.

The landscape blurred around her, fields of corn and alfalfa rushing past like a river of green.

Finally, she was at Ada's house. She jumped out of the buggy and hurried to the house without securing the horse.

"Ada!" Wilma cried as she opened the door and raced inside, her face flushed with concern.

Ada met her in the hallway. "What happened?"

"Red," Wilma sobbed, swallowing hard against the lump in her throat. "A man came and took him away. He said Red was his dog, but he must treat him badly. Red didn't want to go with him, Ada. That man, he was so cruel."

Ada's eyes filled with empathy and was then replaced by fierce determination. "Then we'll get him back, Wilma."

27

"How?" Wilma asked, her voice cracking. "I don't even know where the man lives."

"Oh. Let's not worry about that just yet," Ada replied, her mind already racing with ideas. "First, we need something to offer him. Something that might make him give up Red willingly."

"Like what?" Wilma wiped the tears away. Ada had a plan, and she knew she'd figure it out.

"Money," Ada said, her voice firm. "We'll offer him money in exchange for Red."

"Yes. Good idea. He looked like he didn't have much of anything. How much should we offer?"

"A lot. A bundle of cash, so he can't say no." Ada's eyes narrowed with determination.

"No, Ada! That won't work. We don't have time to go to the bank. We have to do something right now."

"Leave that to me," Ada answered, walking over to her kitchen counter and lifting a ceramic cookie jar shaped like a plump sheep. With a wink, she removed the lid, revealing a thick wad of cash nestled atop the chocolate chip cookies. "I've been saving this for a rainy day. But helping you get Red away from cruelty, well, that's more important than any storm."

"Ada," Wilma breathed, her heart swelling with gratitude. "I'll pay you back."

"Let's just worry about making sure you get Red back, and away from that man."

"Thank you," Wilma whispered, clutching her friend's hand tightly. "Alright, so we have the money, but how are we going to find that man? I don't even know his name. Wait, he said it was Cal."

"Cal?"

"Yes. It must be short for something, but that must be his first name. I don't even know his last name."

"Breathe for a moment and then think."

Wilma gulped in a breath of air.

"How did he know you had Red?" Ada asked.

Wilma's mouth dropped open. "He didn't say."

Ada thought for a moment, her eyes narrowing as she considered who knew about the dog. Finally, she snapped her fingers and looked at Wilma with excitement. "The vet! That's got to be it! Obadiah and Eli took the dog to the vet, didn't they?"

"Of course! They must've given the vet my address," Wilma exclaimed, her eyes widening in realization. "He must have called around to local vets, asking if anyone had treated a dog matching Red's description."

"Exactly," Ada nodded, her warm smile returning. "So, all we need to do is go back to the vet and see if they can give us any information on the man."

Wilma hesitated. "But what if they won't tell us? We could be getting them into trouble if we ask for someone else's information."

"Wilma, dear," Ada said gently, placing a reassuring hand on her friend's shoulder. "This is about bringing Red home. Sometimes, we have to take risks for the sake of those we love. And I know how much you love that dog."

"I wouldn't say love, but you're right, Ada. I'll do whatever it takes to bring Red back to me, but only because the owner was treating him badly. If that means asking the vet for help, then so be it."

"Good!" Ada clapped, her rosy cheeks glowing with determination. "Now, let's get going. The sooner we find out where that man lives, the sooner we can bring Red home. I'll leave Samuel a note and tell him where I've gone."

Wilma waited while Ada wrote the note. It felt like an eternity.

"Thank you, Ada," Wilma whispered as they headed out the door. "I don't know what I would do without you."

"Neither do I, Wilma, neither do I."

They climbed into the buggy, ready to face whatever challenges lay ahead in their quest to find Red.

CHAPTER 6

Wilma, with Ada by her side, drove her horse and buggy down the familiar dirt lanes, each bump in the road doing little to quell the turmoil in Wilma's heart. The foliage blurred past her as she clutched the reins tighter, her knuckles turning white.

"Remember, Wilma," Ada said, breaking the silence, "we're not here to cause any trouble. We just need to find out where that man lives so we can bring Red home."

"Of course."

They pulled up at the veterinarian's office and got out, their feet crunching on the gravel as they approached the door. The bell above the entrance jingled merrily when they entered the building.

"Good morning," Ada greeted the receptionist behind the counter.

"Hello," the receptionist replied.

"We have a bit of an issue," Wilma hesitated for a moment before continuing. "We believe someone found out about my dog, Red, from this office. Someone showed up at my home earlier today and took Red away."

The receptionist looked at her blankly.

"We believe the man's first name is Cal. We were hoping," Ada added, "that you might know him." Ada gave the woman the dog's description and then added, "We just want to talk to this man and see if we can work something out."

The receptionist shifted uncomfortably as if unsure about sharing the information. Then she nodded hesitantly. "I remember the man. He was here this morning. I'm so sorry. I was the one who gave him your address. He had a photo of the dog and said it was his." She bit her lip.

Ada leaned forward. "Please help us. He treated the dog cruelly and is probably beating on him at this very moment. We need that man's address so we can rescue the dog. It is his, but we must rescue it. Please if you're an animal lover…"

"I'm probably going to get fired for this."

Ada stepped closer and said in a low voice. "No one needs to know."

"The man has never brought an animal here to be treated, but I know where he lives. I see him when I drive past. He's known in the area as someone to avoid." The receptionist wrote his address on a piece of paper and handed it over.

"Thank you," Wilma said as she took the paper and looked down at it. "You've been very helpful."

"Good luck," the receptionist said as they left.

With renewed urgency, they climbed back into the buggy. Ada unfolded the street map to guide Wilma to their destination.

The modest home loomed before them, its peeling paint and unkempt yard a testament to the man's disregard for what was under his care.

Despite her apprehension, Wilma took a deep breath, gathered her courage, and knocked on the door with Ada standing by her side.

The door creaked open, revealing the man who had taken Red. His eyes flicked between the two women, an irritated sneer forming on his lips. "What do you want?"

"Hello," Wilma began, trying to keep her voice steady, "we've come about Red, the dog you took from me today."

The man scoffed, rolling his eyes. "That mangy mutt took off not long after I got him back 'ere."

Wilma's heart plummeted, a cold dread gripping her as she exchanged a worried glance with Ada. Surely he couldn't be telling the truth... could he?

"Wait," Wilma said, her voice firmer now as she stared into the man's cold eyes. "You expect us to believe that Red just ran off?"

The man crossed his arms defensively, scowling at her. "I don't care what you believe, lady. He bolted first chance he got. Now if you don't mind, I've got better things to do than stand 'ere talking about some worthless hound."

"Red is not worthless," Wilma retorted, anger bubbling up inside her. She glanced at Ada, who gave her an encouraging nod before turning back to the man.

"We're willing to pay you for him. Name your price," Ada said.

"Pay me?" The man snorted in derision, his eyes narrowing as he looked them up and down. "Look, you two clearly don't know a thing about dogs. That mutt ain't worth a dime. Now get off my property before I call the cops."

"Please," Wilma implored, desperation lacing her voice. "We just want Red back."

"Enough!" the man bellowed, his face reddening with anger. "I told you the dog is gone! Now leave me alone!" With that, he slammed the door in their faces, the force of it rattling the windows.

CHAPTER 7

*W*ilma stared at the closed door, her heart pounding in her chest. She could feel tears prickling at the corners of her eyes, but she willed herself not to cry.

Not yet.

There had to be something they could do, some way to find Red and bring him home.

"Wilma," Ada said softly, placing a hand on her arm. "Come on, let's go back to the buggy. We'll figure something out."

Numbly, Wilma nodded, her mind racing with thoughts of Red and the cruel man who had taken him. As they climbed into the buggy and began their journey home, she couldn't shake the feeling that she had failed Red somehow.

"Ada," she whispered, tears finally flowing down her

cheeks. "What are we going to do? Do you think that man's telling the truth?"

"I don't know, Wilma. I think so, otherwise he would've taken the money. We might come across him while we're driving back."

As they rode through the countryside, Wilma clung to Ada's words like a lifeline. She would not let this be the end of their story. Somehow, someway, she would make sure that Red was safe and loved no matter what it took.

The clatter of horse hooves on the dirt road echoed in the air as Wilma guided the buggy back home.

"Wilma," Ada said gently, breaking the silence that had settled between them. "I know this is hard, but we'll figure something out to find him."

Wilma sighed, feeling a knot forming in her throat. "I just... I never thought I'd get so upset about a dog," she admitted, her voice barely above a whisper. "I didn't even want one. I never wanted a dog."

Ada glanced over at her, offering a small smile. "Well, Red found a way into your heart, didn't he?"

A faint laugh escaped Wilma's lips— a mix of sadness and fondness. "I don't think so. I wouldn't have minded if he had a nice owner. I would've been happy for them to be reunited. You should've seen Red with that man, Ada. He was terrified."

"We'll find him and bring him home."

Wilma looked at the road ahead, her thoughts consumed by memories of Red, the way he looked at her, the way he gulped his food in one go, and how he always looked up into her face.

"Ada, what if..." her voice faltered for a moment before she continued, "What if we can't find him? What if he's lost or hurt?"

"We will find him."

Wilma blinked back tears and straightened her posture. "You're right, Ada. Thank you."

"Of course," Ada replied, smiling warmly. "Now, let's think about something else. I'll make you a nice breakfast, and then we'll come up with a plan. I'll make a sign to put on the shop's door. Hopefully someone will have seen him."

"Okay."

As they approached the orchard, Wilma couldn't help but feel a pang of despair, knowing Red was out there alone. They would find him, she vowed silently. They had to.

"I have to work on the shop today."

"On it or in it?"

"I have to stock it with food so we can put the sign out and open it for business too."

"Okay. That would take our mind off things."

"We have to try everything. I also want to go back where we were and look around the streets," Wilma said.

Ada nodded. "Good idea. Let's do that."

CHAPTER 8

*F*avor lay on the couch, cocooned in her favorite quilt, as she carefully guided her needle through the fabric, bringing to life a delicate floral pattern on the sampler. The needlework was a thoughtful gift from Harriet, who had brought it to keep Favor occupied during her recovery.

Before Favor could react, Cherish burst into the house like a whirlwind, causing her to jump with surprise. "Cherish! You startled me," Favor exclaimed, her heart still racing.

With a playful grin, Cherish scooted over and plopped down next to Favor, her eyes immediately drawn to the sewing project. "Your stitches are so even, Favor. I wish I could make mine look that neat. So, you're feeling better?" she asked, her concern evident in her voice.

"I am." Favor then whispered, "Harriet knows."

"Knows what?" Cherish whispered back.

"About the baby."

Cherish's mouth fell open. "You didn't tell her before you told *Mamm,* did you?"

Favor shook her head. "Of course not. She guessed."

"And then you told her?"

"I had to. Melvin doesn't know yet, but I'll have to tell him soon too."

"I mean and then you told *Mamm.* Please tell me you've told her."

"No. Don't make me feel bad about it."

"I'm not. It's just that she'd want to be the first to know, after you told me, of course."

"I didn't mean to tell anyone. I'll tell *Mamm* soon. Don't nag at me."

Cherish leaned back. "Wow. Those hormones are kicking in already."

Favor frowned at her. "I don't like being pushed to tell everyone when I'm not ready."

"Okay. I won't say another thing."

The scents of cinnamon and cocoa filled the house, accompanying the gentle clattering of pots and pans from the kitchen. Cherish heard Harriet humming a melody.

"That smells good. What's she cooking?" Cherish asked.

"A chocolate cake. It's my favorite, and Simon's too."

"Harriet is quite generous, isn't she? You're truly

blessed to have her care for you like this. I haven't even met Malachi's mother yet. She won't be fussing over me when I'm pregnant."

"I never thought I'd say this, but she's been wonderful since she got here."

"Favor, when are you going to tell *Mamm?*"

Favor frowned at Cherish. "Stop it. You said you weren't going to say any more about it."

"Think how upset she'll be, then you'll get upset and then Simon will get upset—"

"I wanted to wait until I'm three months along, Cherish," she confessed. "But it's getting harder and harder to keep this a secret."

"You won't be able to do it."

"This is different from any other secret I've kept. Now Harriet's guessed and that's kind of ruined my plans." Favor looked back down at the project to take her mind off the struggles of secret-keeping. Her fingers delicately pulled the needle and thread through the fabric, her eyes intent on making each stitch the same size.

"Let's be honest, Favor," Cherish teased, watching her sister work. "You've never been able to keep a secret for very long."

Favor chuckled sheepishly, knowing her sister was right. Secrets had always felt like a caged bird longing to be set free. "That's true. I just don't want to disappoint anyone, you know?"

"Disappoint?" Cherish shook her head, her voice

laced with disbelief. "Favor, this is wonderful news! Everyone will be overjoyed."

Favor took a deep breath, her thoughts swirling. "Like you said, *Mamm* will find out that you knew, and that Harriet knew before she knew."

"Maybe just tell people close to you and ask them to keep it quiet."

Favor thought about that for a while. "If I tell *Mamm,* she'll have to tell Ada. They don't keep secrets from each other."

"Hmm, and then Debbie and Krystal will overhear them talking about it,

and they'll find out too."

Favor nodded. "I guess some secrets aren't meant to be kept. Simon and I will tell Melvin tonight."

"Really?" Cherish's face lit up. "Are you sure?"

"Positive," Favor replied, her resolve strengthening.

"Then what about *Mamm?*"

Favor's brow furrowed as she contemplated the order of events. "No wait, I have to tell her first. What do you think?"

Cherish took a moment to ponder the question, her gaze drifting toward the kitchen wondering when the cake would be ready. Finally, she spoke, her words measured and thoughtful. "It's really up to you, Favor. Both families are going to be thrilled either way, when-ever you tell them. I'm just pleased I was the first to know."

Favor bit her lip, the weight of the decision pressing

down on her. She knew that both her mother and Harriet had been looking forward to this moment for some time, but she couldn't shake the feeling that there was a proper order to things. Her thoughts raced, considering the implications of her choices. "Maybe tomorrow I'll go to your house and call *Mamm*."

"Okay. I guess she won't need to know that your in-laws found out first. I'll see if Harriet needs help with that cake. I'm great at making frosting, possibly the world's best frosting creator." Cherish got up and headed to the kitchen.

Favor smiled at her sister's comment. She always announced how good she was at everything.

Cherish walked into the kitchen, and Harriet looked over at her and smiled. "Good morning, Harriet. Please don't tell me you've started making the frosting."

Harriet chuckled. "No, not yet. I still have to let the cake cool before I even think about frosting. But if you're offering to help, I won't say no."

Cherish grinned and rolled up her sleeves, ready to get to work. As she started mixing together the ingredients for the frosting, she couldn't help but think about Favor's secret. She knew how hard it was to keep something like that to herself, especially when it was such exciting news.

"Harriet, do you think Favor should tell *Mamm* before Melvin finds out?"

Harriet paused for a moment, staring at Cherish.

"You know that I know?"

"I do. I just don't want *Mamm* to be upset. I would be if I was the last to find out."

"I think that's up to Favor. It's a delicate situation, and she'll have to think about it. There's no rush to tell Melvin, and your mother will understand."

Cherish nodded, understanding the complexity of the situation. "I just want to make sure she doesn't feel pressured one way or the other."

Harriet frowned at Cherish. "Do you think I'm pressuring her?"

"No, not at all. I just know that Favor has always had a hard time making decisions without feeling like she's letting someone down. This is her news to share, and I just want to make sure she feels comfortable doing so in her own time."

Harriet smiled softly, her eyes reflecting understanding. "Every young woman faces moments of tough decisions, especially when it involves family. Favor will figure it out."

Cherish was thoughtful while she mixed, tasted and then spread the frosting onto the cake. "I hope, one day, Malachi and I will have some good news to share. It would be wonderful if my children and Favor's could grow up together."

"It will happen." Harriet paused, her hands still, and looked deeply into Cherish's eyes. "Life is filled with surprises and blessings. I never thought the day would come that I'd be a grandmother. Your good news will come too."

CHAPTER 9

Favor sat beneath her living room window as it was casting a golden glow on the quilted fabric that lay in Favor's lap. The gentle rhythm of her needlework provided a soothing backdrop as she and Cherish chatted quietly over way too much chocolate cake.

When Harriet left the room to start on the evening meal, Cherish whispered to Favor, "Wow. It's like you have your own personal cook."

"I know. It has been good. She'll be a great help when the baby arrives. She can change all the dirty diapers." The thought brought a mischievous grin to her face, and she glanced sideways at Cherish, who chuckled in response.

"That's true. Well, I guess I should be getting back home. Malachi will be wondering where I've been. He'll understand when I tell him I stayed for the cake."

"It's a shame there's none left for him. You could've taken him a piece home."

"Hmm, maybe I won't tell him about it."

They both laughed, and then Cherish stood up and yelled out goodbye to Harriet.

"Bye, Cherish, and thanks for the frosting. It was delicious," came the reply.

"You're welcome," Cherish responded as she walked to the door.

Favor got up and opened the door for her. "I can always count on you for some laughs."

"Anytime, Favor," Cherish replied, giving her a quick kiss on her cheek.

Once she was gone, Favor returned to the couch and pulled the quilt over her and then she dozed off.

The sun was just setting as Simon's familiar footsteps approached the house. The sound of his heavy boots echoed through the still evening air, announcing his presence before he even entered the room.

"Ah, there you are," Simon said, his eyes lighting up as they fell upon Favor, who was just opening her eyes. "How was your day?"

"Much better now that you're home," Favor replied as she sat up. "Simon, we need to talk about something important."

"Of course. What is it?" Simon asked, concern etching his features as he settled himself beside her.

"Cherish was here earlier, and we spoke about... well, about when we should tell your parents the news,"

Favor began. "I think it's time. They've been so kind and helpful, especially Ma, and I don't think we should keep it a secret from Pa for any longer."

Simon chuckled. "Okay."

"I don't want everyone to know, only close family."

"They're going back to their house soon. Do you want to tell them before they go?"

"Yes."

"I'll get them."

Once the older couple were seated in front of Favor, she began, her voice barely audible in the quiet room. "Simon and I have some news we'd like to share with you."

Melvin's eyes widened, and he clasped his hands together, as if bracing himself for the revelation. "What is it?"

"We're expecting a baby," Simon announced, his strong voice carrying the weight of the moment.

"Really? A grandchild?" Melvin exclaimed, his face lighting up with pure joy. "I had no idea. No idea at all." Melvin grinned at his wife.

Favor bit her lip, a flicker of doubt crossing her mind. Could Harriet have told him? But before she could dwell on the thought, Melvin enveloped her in a warm embrace, his congratulations filling the air.

"Ah, our family is growing," Melvin said with a smile, his happiness evident even as Favor questioned the sincerity of his surprise. But for now, reveling in the shared excitement of their impending arrival was enough, and Favor let herself become swept up in the excitement.

Melvin wiped a tear from his eye, the emotion overwhelming him. "You know," he began, his voice cracking slightly, "I spoke with the bishop today. He's given us permission to buy that land next door."

"Really?" Favor asked.

"Yes. Our family will have more room to grow, and our farm will prosper for generations to come," Melvin added.

Favor glanced around the cozy kitchen, picturing the pitter-patter of little feet running through the hallways and the laughter of children echoing within the walls. She imagined teaching her girls needlework by the fireplace, just as her much older stepsister Florence and her mother had taught her.

"Simon, your father and I are so pleased for both of you," Harriet said, her beaming smile warming the room. "We've always hoped for this day to come, and now it's finally here."

"Thank you, Ma," Simon replied.

Harriet and Melvin left a few minutes later, and Simon and Favor sat down to eat the food Harriet had prepared.

They said their silent prayers as usual and then as they ate, Favor's thoughts drifted to the future.

"Are you okay?" Simon asked, noticing her faraway expression.

"I'm just thinking about what's coming next for us," she replied, a smile still on her lips.

"Me too," he said, reaching for her hand across the table. "I can't wait to see you as a mother. You'll be amazing."

"I hope so," she said, feeling a flutter of nerves. "I just want everything to be perfect."

"It will be. We'll make sure of it," he said.

CHAPTER 10

*I*n the stillness of Cherish's barn, Favor walked over to call her mother. The barn, usually bustling with activity, was now enveloped in a hush.

Cherish handed the phone to Favor, its old-fashioned rotary dial looking out of place among the traditional Amish surroundings. It was one of the few concessions the family had made to modernity, especially for emergencies.

"Just don't mention Harriet or Melvin," Cherish said.

Taking a deep breath, Favor dialed her mother's number. The line buzzed for a few moments before a familiar voice answered, "Hello?"

"*Mamm*, it's Favor."

"Ah, Favor! It's been so long since we spoke. How are you?"

"I'm well, *Mamm*. There's something I want to share with you," Favor began, her voice quivering with a mix of excitement and apprehension.

Wilma sensed her daughter's hesitance. "Is everything alright, Favor?"

"Yes, everything's fine. Better than fine, actually," Favor said, gathering courage. "*Mamm*, after all these years of praying and waiting, Simon and I are expecting a baby."

The line was silent for a heartbeat, and then Wilma's voice returned, choked with emotion, "Oh, Favor, that's *wunderbaar*! Blessed be the Lord! I've prayed for this day."

Tears welled in Favor's eyes as she felt the weight of her mother's love and joy. "Thank you, *Mamm*. It's a dream come true for both of us."

However, as the conversation flowed, Favor's excitement overrode her caution. "Harriet has been so supportive since she found out. She's even started knitting tiny booties."

Cherish gasped and shook her head, but it was too late; the words were out.

There was a momentary pause. "Harriet knows?" Wilma's voice, although gentle, held a hint of hurt.

Favor's heart sank as she realized her slip. "Yes, *Mamm*, only because she guessed because I was sick. She asked and I had to tell her. I did want to wait."

"And Melvin?" Wilma asked.

"He knows too," Favor admitted softly.

Cherish grabbed the phone's receiver out of Favor's hand. "They only know because Harriet guessed. She had to tell him because his wife knew."

"Cherish? You knew too?"

Cherish bit her lip. "I guessed too. She wasn't going to tell me. I'll put Favor back on."

"I'm back again," Favor said to her mother while shaking her head at Cherish.

Wilma sighed deeply on the other end. "I understand, Favor. I'm not upset. I'm just surprised, but it doesn't matter who found out first. The important thing is that you'll soon be a mother."

"I know. I really did want to tell you first."

"She did," Cherish said into the phone.

"I'm sorry, *Mamm.*"

Wilma's voice softened, "It's alright, Favor. There's nothing to be sorry about. I'm so happy. We've all been waiting for this."

Favor nodded, wiping away a tear. "Of course, *Mamm.* I'm not far along. I didn't want to let anyone know until I was three months. Could you keep the news to yourself for now?"

"Of course. I won't tell anyone."

"You can tell Ada, but no one else and tell her the same."

"I'll tell her. Ada will be delighted that you've let her in on the news."

"How are things there, *Mamm?*"

Wilma thought about Red. That incident with that

man taking Red away had been consuming her thoughts, but she didn't want to worry her daughter about that. "Fine, just fine. It'll be the first day of harvest tomorrow and everything is buzzing along. We've also opened the shop and Ada and I are organizing an apple pie contest for charity."

"That sounds like fun. Oh, I miss being there."

"Me too," Cherish said into the phone.

"It would be nice if you both still lived here, but you're both happy and that makes me happy. Have you been well, Favor?"

"I had some morning sickness, but it only lasted about a week. I'm hoping it doesn't come back. It's the worst."

"I'm pleased you've got people there to watch over you."

"I do. I have both friends and family here."

Wilma chuckled lightly. "Sounds like you've got everyone by your side. You always did attract a crowd, Favor."

Cherish overheard and snickered in the background, and Favor shot her a playful glare. "Well, Cherish has been the biggest help, *Mamm.* She's like my second shadow now. Always has advice for every situation, and as you know she's the best at everything."

Cherish piped up, "Well, someone has to make sure you're eating more than just chocolate cake!"

Favor laughed. "You were the one who ate all the cake."

Wilma laughed along with them. "Was that a craving, Favor? I remember when I was expecting you, I couldn't get enough of beets and buttermilk."

Favor made a face. "Oh, *Mamm,* that sounds awful!"

"Everyone's taste is different, dear," Wilma replied.

Cherish leaned into the phone again. "Don't worry, *Mamm.* I'll keep a close eye on her. And I promise not to guess any more secrets!"

Wilma chuckled. "Well, that's good to know. You two always were a handful when you got together."

The sisters exchanged grins, memories of their shared escapades bringing a glow to their faces.

Favor's voice softened. "Thank you, *Mamm,* for understanding. We love you."

"We do," Cherish added.

"And I love both of you with all my heart. Keep looking out for each other, alright?"

"We will," they chorused.

With a few more pleasantries exchanged, the call eventually came to an end. Wilma replaced the phone's receiver and looked around the barn. She'd come there to get something and now it had left her mind completely. But whatever it was, it didn't matter.

She couldn't wait to tell Ada the good news.

Making her way back to the house to find Ada, Wilma reflected on the unpredictable turns of life. She had been grappling with her feelings about Obadiah and Red, but now, a ray of joy had pierced through.

Life was ever shifting and full of surprises.

CHAPTER 11

*E*ntering the house, Wilma was greeted by the aromatic scent of fresh baking. Ada was carefully rolling out a pie crust. Flour dusted her face and apron.

Wilma tried to control her excitement as she approached, not wanting to startle her. "Ada, you'll never guess what I just heard."

Ada looked up, her face full of curiosity. "What is it, Wilma? You seem like you've just found a hidden treasure in the barn."

Taking a deep breath, Wilma whispered, "Favor's expecting. She's going to have a baby."

The rolling pin slipped from Ada's grasp, landing on the floor with a thud and sending a small cloud of flour into the air. Ada's eyes widened in disbelief. "Really? After all this time? Oh, bless her heart!"

Wilma nodded, her eyes moist. "Yes. It's been such a journey for her and Simon. I'm overjoyed."

Ada reached out to embrace her friend, but in her excitement, she managed to knock a bowl off the counter. The crash was loud, and they both jumped, then burst into peals of laughter.

"I'm so thrilled I'm causing a ruckus in your kitchen!" Ada exclaimed, trying to regain her composure. She bent down to clean up the mess. "We'll need to start planning a baby quilt, and oh, the baby clothes. We'll need to make her lots of them."

Wilma smiled, wiping away a tear. "Yes, and we will. We'll have plenty of time though because she said it's early days. That's why she doesn't want us to tell anybody else."

Ada's eyebrows rose. "She doesn't mind me knowing?"

"She said I could tell you, but no one else."

Ada smiled and resumed picking up everything she'd dropped on the floor.

The two women resumed their kitchen activities, but Wilma wasn't as joyful as she should've been.

Ada glanced over at her friend and frowned, noticing the downturned corners of Wilma's mouth. She walked over, her long dress rustling. "We'll find him, Wilma," she reassured her. "We can go looking for him tomorrow."

"Thank you, Ada. I suppose you think I'm silly. It's just that Red has no one to watch out for him. That man is horrible. What if he finds him, or has found him and is treating him cruelly?" Wilma murmured.

"Don't even think about that," Ada said.

"We can't go looking for Red again tomorrow, Ada," she said, regret lacing her voice. "We've got to open the shop."

Ada's warm eyes twinkled with determination as she dusted the flour from her fingers. "Why don't we ask Daphne and Susan to work there, and you can slip away when it's not busy?"

Wilma furrowed her brow, considering the idea. It could work; Daphne and Susan were reliable friends who knew their way around the shop. But was it fair to burden them with additional responsibility?

"Are you sure they won't mind?" Wilma asked.

"Of course not. They'd be happy to help, especially if it means finding Red."

"Alright," Wilma agreed, her voice steady.

"Good. I'll call them both from the barn when I get home. It will all work out, you'll see."

Wilma sent up a silent prayer for Red's safety and then waited while Ada made her a cup of tea.

Ada sat next to her with her own cup while the pie baked in the oven. "It's such good news about Favor."

"I know. Her life will be changed forever."

Ada put the cup up to her lips. "I wonder how many children she'll end up having."

Wilma laughed, grateful for Ada's light-heartedness. "Probably a whole herd of them."

They both giggled at the thought before settling into a comfortable silence, sipping their tea as the scent of fresh pie filled the kitchen. The thoughts of Red still lingered in Wilma's mind, but she pushed them aside, determined to enjoy this moment with Ada.

As the timer beeped, Ada stood up to take the pie out of the oven. She carefully lifted it with oven mitts, placing it on the counter to cool. The aroma of the pie was heavenly, and Wilma felt her mouth water.

"Would you like a slice?" Ada asked, already reaching for a knife.

Wilma nodded eagerly as Ada began to cut a generous slice for both of them. The crust was flaky and buttery, and the filling was perfectly sweetened with just the right amount of tartness.

"This is delicious, Ada," Wilma complimented.

"I know. Shall we hide it from the others?"

Wilma laughed. "I think they'll smell it as soon as they walk in the house."

"Well, we've got dessert. I've been too distracted to think about what else we'll eat. You sit there. When I finish eating this, I'll make a casserole out of leftovers."

Wilma nodded. *"Denke,* Ada."

"It'll be hard to keep the news about Favor quiet."

"I know, but we must." Wilma kept the news to herself that Favor hadn't told her first. It was a little hurtful and surprising that they told Harriet first, but she wouldn't let that ruin her joy about gaining another grandchild.

CHAPTER 12

The next day, Wilma and her friends were working in the shop getting it ready to open.

"Wilma, when are you going to bake your pie for the competition?" Susan asked, her rosy cheeks flushed with excitement.

"Not yet. Where would I have found the time? I plan on finishing mine the day before the contest. How about you?"

"Mine's already baked and ready to go," Ada replied proudly. "I like my crust hard, so I make it a few days before it's meant to be eaten."

"Soft or crunchy crust, that is the question, isn't it?" chimed Daphne as she folded paper bags in readiness for customers.

"I prefer a soft crust, though. It complements the

tender apples so well," Wilma said. "Like the one you made yesterday, Ada."

"Ah, but a crunchy crust holds up better against the juicy filling," countered Ada.

"True, but I find a delicate balance between the two textures makes for the perfect pie," Daphne said.

As they bantered about crusts, some early customers entered the shop. The women quickly shifted their focus back to work, attending to each person with genuine warmth and attentiveness.

Between customers, Wilma pondered her pie recipe. She knew the contest was just a friendly competition, but she couldn't help wanting to win.

Ada still had the competition on her mind. "Whichever pie wins, I think we can all agree that raising money for charity is what counts."

Susan nodded. "And bringing people together over good food is what will make this contest special."

As they all chatted some more about pies, Wilma glanced out the window, her brow furrowed with concern about Red. "Does anyone mind if I leave for a while? I want to drive around to see if I can find Red."

"Of course not, Wilma," Daphne assured her. "We've got things under control here."

"*Jah,* go find that dog of yours," Susan chimed in.

"Would you like some company?" Ada offered. "I could come with you. You can drive, and I'll keep an eye out for Red."

"Thank you, Ada. I'd appreciate that," Wilma said

gratefully. She knew her friend's empathetic nature would be a comfort during their search.

After hitching up their horse and buggy, the two women climbed aboard, with Wilma taking the reins while Ada scanned the streets.

"Are you sure you want to do this, Wilma?" Ada asked softly, her eyes searching her friend's face. "You don't have to keep Red, you know. There are others who might be able to take him in. I mean, if we find him we can still look for a good home, far away from that man."

Wilma sighed, her hands tightening on the reins as her thoughts churned. "I know, Ada," she murmured, "but for reasons I can't quite explain, I feel a connection to that dog. I don't want to let him down. We just have to find him first."

"We'll do our best. That's all we can do," Ada said, turning back to look out the window.

"Maybe Red was meant to teach me something important," Wilma said.

"Or maybe he just needs your love."

"Either way," Wilma said resolutely, "I'm not giving up on him."

CHAPTER 13

*T*he horse and buggy gently swayed as it rolled down the gravel roads, Ada sitting beside Wilma with her eyes scanning their surroundings.

"Wilma," Ada began thoughtfully, leaning into the rhythm of the buggy's movement. "Why don't we knock on doors around Red's owner's home? Someone might have seen him."

Wilma nodded, her hands steady on the reins. "That's a good idea, Ada. But you'll have to do the knocking. You know I'm not much for talking to strangers."

"I don't mind at all."

They stopped at several homes, Ada getting out of the buggy and returning with a shake of her head after each inquiry. The discouragement weighed heavily on

Wilma, but she clung to hope like a lifeline, urging the horse onward.

"Let's try the local vet," Ada suggested, her voice tinged with determination. "Perhaps someone brought Red there."

"I guess it's worth a try," agreed Wilma, steering the horse toward the small veterinary clinic nestled among the town's shops.

Wilma prayed silently, her grip tightening on the reins. When they arrived, Wilma couldn't bring herself to go in. Ada did so and returned a few moments later, her face somber. "No luck," she said softly. "He hasn't been here."

"Then let's ask the folks on the street," Wilma insisted, her desperation mounting. "Someone must have seen him."

After a couple more hours, they'd had enough of searching.

"Let's head home," Ada finally suggested. "We've done all we can for today."

Wilma nodded, tears prickling at the corners of her eyes. She knew Ada was right, but it pained her to give up without finding Red. As she turned the buggy toward home, she couldn't help but feel a sense of defeat settling over her like a heavy blanket.

"Maybe I wasn't meant to keep him," she whispered, her heart aching with loss. "I was trying to avoid feeling like this. That's why I let Obadiah go. I don't like getting attached to someone and then going through this pain."

"It's just a dog, Wilma."

"No. You're wrong. He was a friend. A companion."

The rest of the drive home was spent in silence. Coming up the driveway, they saw that the shop's door was closed.

"They must've gone home already," Wilma said staring at the shop.

"It's late, Wilma."

As they pulled up back at Wilma's house, she felt helpless. The thought of coming home without Red made her heart sink.

After they unhitched the buggy and rubbed down the horse, the two women entered the house together, both feeling the weight of the day's failure on their shoulders.

As Wilma set about preparing dinner, Ada tried to keep the conversation light. But the two women couldn't help but feel the sorrow in the room.

It wasn't long before the silence became too much for Wilma. "I want him back, Ada. It breaks my heart to think of him wandering out there alone and hungry. He probably thought his lonely sad days were over. It must be a nightmare for poor Red."

Ada nodded sympathetically. "I know, but we have to be realistic. Red could be anywhere by now. We've searched far and wide, and there's only so much we can do."

Wilma wiped away tears that had begun to trail down her cheeks. "I just can't give up hope," she said softly. "He's out there somewhere, and I have to find him."

"Okay," Ada said gently. "Then we'll keep looking. We'll put up posters and spread the word. We won't stop until he's found. Stop what you're doing. I'll make you a nice cup of tea and we'll enjoy some cookies before we start cooking."

A small smile tugged at Wilma's lips. She knew she could always count on Ada to support her, no matter what. "Thank you," she whispered.

CHAPTER 14

*I*t was the first day of the apple harvest and excitement hung in the air.

Over the next few weeks, there would be so many visitors to the orchard, from seasonal workers to trucks loading up on apples, to family and friends coming to help.

Then there was the cookout they always enjoyed on the evening of the first day of harvest. All the workers would join in for the feast.

Wilma and Ada would be kept busy all day preparing the food.

Ada had said she would be there early, so Wilma took her morning coffee out onto the porch to wait for her. The sun had just peeked over the horizon, so it was still only early, but not too early for Fairfax and Matthew, who were there to oversee everything.

She gave them a wave. Matthew didn't see her, but

Fairfax smiled and waved back. As soon as Wilma settled into a chair, there was a rustle in the bushes around the house. Immediately, she got to her feet, hoping it was Red.

There was nothing to see. Wilma sat down again, figuring the noise to be either her imagination or a sudden gust of wind.

By the time she heard stirrings within the house, there was still no Ada. With her coffee finished, she went inside to make everyone breakfast. There would be no cooked breakfast today apart from toast.

After everyone had eaten, Debbie and Krystal had offered to do the washing up, but Wilma insisted she'd do it. Jared was anxious for his mother to join him in helping Matthew, and Wilma knew Krystal wanted to go outside and wait for Jed. Both Krystal and Debbie had found people to work for them, so they could help at the orchard.

Just as Wilma had finished drying the last dish, she looked outside and saw Florence making her way to the house. She was carrying her newborn baby and Iris was part walking and part skipping alongside.

Wilma was delighted to see the baby once more. She wiped her hands on a towel and hurried out the back door.

She waved to Florence and caught her attention. "Come on up, Florence," Wilma called out, her voice full of affection. "It's been too long since you've visited."

"Thank you, Wilma. I couldn't miss out on the first

day of harvest. This is Chess's first harvest. He won't remember it, but I'll tell him about it."

Iris ran ahead and hugged Wilma's legs. "Hello, Iris. Have you come to help with the harvest too?"

"No. Mom said I have to keep out of the way."

Wilma laughed. "I'm sure we can find something for you to do."

Florence saw Wilma staring at the baby. "Do you want to hold him?"

"Yes."

Florence gave a laugh and handed the baby over. "I hope my little one doesn't cause too much trouble during harvest time."

Wilma looked down at him and saw him sleeping peacefully. "I'm sure this little one will never be any trouble to anyone."

"He can't do anything yet," Iris said. "He's too little for me to play with."

"It won't be long, and he'll be able to play with you," Wilma told her.

More people were arriving all the time, but still, there was no Ada.

"We're set. Ada should be here shortly, and both Daphne and Susan promised to pitch in later." Suddenly, Matthew's voice echoed, beckoning everyone to gather round.

Florence, with a playful smirk, whispered, "Let's see how he manages."

Wilma nodded in agreement. "Shall we move closer?"

"Of course," Florence replied, then glanced at the baby in Wilma's arms. "Are you okay with him?"

Wilma hugged him a little tighter. "He's quite content right here, thank you."

Laughing lightly, Florence agreed, "As you wish." They meandered over to the assembling crowd.

Then Wilma spotted Ada hurrying over, her round face beaming at the sight of Florence, Iris and the baby. "Well, if it isn't our favorite *Englisher!*" she exclaimed, giving Florence a gentle hug.

"Hello, Aunt Ada," Iris squawked.

Ada looked down. "Hello, Iris."

"Hello, Ada," Florence said warmly. "It's nice to see you again."

"Everyone's gathering down by the trees. Someone's put Matthew in charge today," Ada informed them.

Wilma didn't say anything negative about Matthew. She was just glad that he'd stopped camping on her porch.

They stood at the edge of the crowd and watched Matthew climb onto the end of a wagon. He got the crowd's attention and started talking.

Firstly, he welcomed everyone to this year's harvest. Then to Wilma's surprise he went on to give a little speech about the history of the orchard. Wilma wasn't prepared for that and had to blink hard so she wouldn't cry. Matthew then went on to explain the proper technique for picking apples and identifying which ones were ripe enough to keep. "Watch me closely now," he instructed, his voice confident yet friendly. "You want to twist and pull just like this." He demonstrated, plucking a shiny red apple from a low-hanging branch.

"Since when did Matthew become such an expert?" Ada whispered playfully to Wilma.

Wilma grinned and whispered back, "He's worked with Fairfax for ages now. I'm glad he's learned something in all that time."

Ada looked over at Krystal, who was standing next to Jed. "But I reckon Matthew's trying to impress someone."

"Krystal, you mean?" Wilma asked,

"Yes, but it's too late. Krystal and Jed go together like salt and pepper. Ambitious Jed with his tour business," Ada grinned.

Wilma watched Matthew some more. "He seems so grown up now that he's living back at his place."

Ada stifled a chuckle. "He's doing a fine job."

"Maybe he'll win Krystal back after all," Wilma whispered back.

"No. Don't forget the salt and pepper. Krystal and Matthew are more like salt and... Hmmm. I can't think of anything that doesn't go with salt."

"Salt doesn't go with sweet things."

"What about salted caramel?"

"Ah, that's true."

Ada nodded toward Krystal and Jed. "Look at them,

Wilma. They're already talking of marriage. Such a good couple. Life has a funny way of working itself out. She was upset about Matthew, went to Cherish's farm to clear her head and then she met Jed."

"True words, Ada," Wilma agreed, her warm smile returning. "We never know what God has planned. I was upset too and then I learned about Favor."

"Shh! It's a secret, remember?" Ada said, looking around.

"It's all right, no one can hear."

Florence stepped closer. "What's this about Favor?"

Ada frowned at Wilma. "See?"

Wilma sighed. "I'll have to tell you now."

"Yes, tell me," Florence insisted.

"She's having a baby."

Florence's face lit up. "Favor is?"

Wilma nodded.

"That's such good news."

"But no one is supposed to know for a while. Please keep it quiet. She wants to wait for a couple of months."

"I understand, but do you think she'd mind if I told Carter?"

Wilma thought about that for a moment. "As long as he doesn't tell anyone."

Ada looked down, shaking her head. "You might as well tell everyone and tell them not to tell anyone."

"I'm sure Favor wouldn't mind me telling Florence."

Ada didn't say any more.

When they looked up, Matthew was almost finished talking.

He ended with, "Now let's get to work. These apples won't pick themselves." Then he jumped off the wagon.

"Come on, Wilma, we better get started making lunch for all these people. They'll be hungry in no time."

Wilma turned to Florence and handed back the baby. "What will you do?"

"Iris and I will stay for a few more minutes and then we'll go home. We'll come back later."

"Very well. Will you be at the cookout tonight?"

"I don't think so. It'll be too hard with Chess."

"Why can't I go, Mom," Iris whined.

"You can when you're older."

Iris huffed.

CHAPTER 15

rystal looked up from placing apples in a bucket, wiping sweat from her brow and smiled at Jed, who was working on the next tree along. He returned the smile, his dark eyes gleaming with the confidence that had drawn her to him.

"It's amazing how quickly these apples have grown," Krystal called out, lifting a large specimen into the sunlight for him to see. She admired its red hue, imagining the juicy sweetness of each bite.

"I'll have to take your word on that! I've never had much to do with orchards, but I do find the whole thing fascinating. Each day I'm learning more."

"Enough to tell your customers on Friday?"

"Yes. At least I'll know more than they do, I hope." Jed stepped closer to Krystal and brushed a couple of strands of hair away from her face. While he was doing that, Matthew appeared out of nowhere, an empty box in his arms.

"Krystal, Jed," Matthew said through clenched teeth. "Don't you think we should focus on picking the apples? There's much work to be done."

"Of course, Matthew," Krystal replied, stifling her irritation at his intrusion. She couldn't help but notice the way his gaze lingered on her, filled with an intensity that unnerved her. But she wouldn't allow him to ruin her day.

"Matthew has a point, Krystal," Jed conceded, his voice placating. "We'll have plenty of time to enjoy the fruits of our labor later."

Krystal frowned at him, and Jed gave her a little wink when Matthew wasn't looking.

"Carry on," Matthew said, still staring at the two of them.

Krystal looked past Matthew when she saw a yellow school bus pulling into the orchard.

"Ah, the school children are here!" Matthew said. "I'll show them around and teach them about our harvest. I'll give them a *proper* tour." With that, he strode off.

Jed didn't say anything, but Krystal knew he was upset about him mentioning a 'proper' tour as though Jed's tours weren't going to be any good.

Then they heard Matthew's loud voice above everyone else.

"Welcome to The Baker Apple Orchard, my young friends! Today, you'll learn how we cultivate and harvest these delicious fruits!"

Krystal looked over for a while and then went back to collecting the apples. "I'm not sure why he's doing that. It's normally Florence who shows the children around."

"She probably can't do it with the new baby and all."

"I know, but why let him do it? It should be Fairfax."

Jed shrugged. "Dunno. Just ignore him."

"Gladly."

IT WAS mid-afternoon when Jared walked up the driveway with Toby, one of his young friends. Toby's father was helping in the orchard. Toby saw his father and went one way while Jared found his mother.

"Hey, Jared," Debbie greeted with a warm smile. "How did you cope with your first day walking home?"

"It was okay." Jared's face scrunched as he looked around.

"What are you looking for?"

"There's no corn!"

Debbie furrowed her brow, confused. "Corn? What are you talking about?"

He let out a sigh, his small hands clenched at his sides. "I learned about harvest at school today. The teacher said it's when you gather crops from the fields. But when I looked around, there's no corn here, *Mamm*. It's not a proper harvest."

Debbie's heart softened as she realized the cause of her son's frustration. She kneeled to his eye level, tenderly brushing a strand of hair from his forehead. "I see why you're upset. But you know, our harvest here is different. We gather apples from our orchard, not corn."

"But why isn't there corn, *Mamm?*" Jared persisted, his eyes filling with disappointment.

"There are all different kinds of harvest. Here at the orchard, we have apple trees so we harvest the apples. If we had corn fields, we'd harvest the corn."

Jared pondered this for a moment, his furrowed brows slowly relaxing. "So, apples are our harvest?"

"Yes, exactly! We have apples, and that's what we work hard to gather during this season. Just like how other farms may have corn or wheat or other crops."

"I'll have to tell the teacher she was wrong."

"I don't think she made a mistake. She was probably talking about corn and later she might talk about different harvests."

"I'm still gonna tell her, but I'll do it in a nice way, so she won't get upset."

Debbie was sure the teacher wouldn't mind. "Do you want to help me pick some apples?"

"Can I have milk and cookies first?"

Debbie smiled. "Sure. Wilma and Ada are in the kitchen. They'll be able to fix you something."

Jared turned and ran to the house.

CHAPTER 16

*A*s the sun dipped below the horizon, the evening gathered its warm glow from large gas torches. Along with those, Samuel and the men lit up the night with overhead lights, while a crackling fire drew friends and neighbors together. Amidst the chatter, Ada and Wilma were in the kitchen putting the last touches on the salads.

Ada's eyes wandered to the kitchen window, where an unfamiliar figure caught her attention. "Wilma, do you see that man?" she whispered, nodding discreetly toward a tall, broad-shouldered stranger. His dark hair spilled over his forehead, and an undeniable aura of confidence surrounded him.

Wilma squinted, trying to make out the newcomer's features. "I can't say that I recognize him," she admitted. "He must be visiting from another community."

"Or maybe he's a wanderer," Ada mused, her eyes twinkling with mischief. "Wouldn't that be intriguing?"

Wilma chuckled and shook her head. "Oh, Ada, always the matchmaker! But who would you pair him with? Debbie and Krystal are already betrothed, and we have no more unmarried daughters. Let's finish our work before diving into speculations about handsome strangers."

"Alright, you've got a point," Ada conceded, returning to her task. Yet, as she stepped outside, her curiosity got the better of her, stealing glances at the man to see what he was up to.

As the last rays of sunlight vanished, work gave way to a communal feast. Samuel and Eli took charge of the cookout, their delicious creations quickly disappearing from the table. Amidst the joyous gathering, the women's thoughts still lingered on the stranger, wondering about the mystery surrounding him.

Ada couldn't resist the urge. "Maybe one of us should go and introduce ourselves, ask him his name," she suggested, taking a plate for herself.

"I don't think that's our place. He could be a guest of someone here." Wilma looked at the food and wasn't the slightest bit hungry; she'd been nibbling all day.

"Of course, you're right," Ada agreed. "Still, I can't help but wonder what or who brought him here."

"We'll find out soon enough. For now, let us focus on the other guests."

"I can do both." Ada popped a small potato into her mouth.

Glad to be off their feet, Ada and Wilma sat down at one of the tables.

"Wilma, just go up and ask him where he's from," Ada insisted, her eyes fixed on the stranger. "I'm sure he won't mind. Look, he's being very helpful loading those apples into that truck. Tell him to have a rest and come and eat something."

"Ada, I already told you I don't feel comfortable doing that," Wilma replied.

"Fine," Ada huffed, shaking her head. "But I still think we should find out more about him."

Krystal approached them. "Wilma, what can I do to help?"

"Thank you," Wilma replied, smiling. "There's nothing to do yet until everyone is finished eating, and then you can help take the plates to the house. There will be loads of washing up to do."

"Sure. I'll have Jed help too."

Ada looked around. "Where is Jed?"

Krystal looked around too. "He was here a moment ago. There he is."

He grinned at her and waved her over, pointing to a plate beside him. "This is yours," Jed told her when she got closer.

"Oh," she said with a laugh, and then she sat beside him. "Thanks." As she started to eat, she noticed he seemed distracted. "Is everything alright?"

"Uh, yeah, it's just..." Jed's voice trailed off as he continued to gaze at the same spot.

Krystal followed his line of sight and saw the stranger. "Who is that man? Do you know him?"

"I do."

Seeing he bore an uncanny resemblance to Jed, she joined the dots. "Jed, is that...?"

"Yeah," Jed confirmed, swallowing hard. "That's Gabe, my older brother. Unfortunately, I have no idea why he's here."

"Your brother?" Krystal asked.

"Yes, my brother," Jed replied, still unable to tear his gaze away from his sibling. "I don't know how he knew I was here. He's probably come to check up on me. Or try to get me to come back. You see, I was supposed to be checking up on Malachi and reporting back to them, but I got sidetracked."

"Maybe you should go talk to him," Krystal suggested gently, placing a comforting hand on his arm.

"Maybe," Jed murmured, his thoughts racing. He knew he needed to face his brother and find out the reason for his unexpected arrival, but the thought of that filled him with dread.

Krystal saw that Jed was bothered. "If that's your brother, you don't seem happy to see him."

"I'm not. I'll talk with him later. Right now, I want to enjoy myself."

CHAPTER 17

*a*mid the joyful gathering, the children played freely, and Jared, familiar with his schoolmates, joined in the fun. But as Debbie immersed herself in conversation, her watchful eyes missed Jared's disappearance.

Panic gripped her heart when she realized Jared was nowhere to be found. Fear surged as she called his name, the minutes stretching into eternity. Community members rallied to help, their prayers seeking divine guidance.

Clutching her apron tightly, Debbie whispered a plea to God, praying for his safety. Wilma's comforting touch reassured her as they continued the search. Just as despair threatened to consume them, a neighbor's voice broke the silence - they found him!

Debbie rushed toward the voice, relief flooding her

soul. There stood Jared, engrossed in conversation with a mysterious man. Grateful for the lady's help, Debbie grabbed Jared's hand, urging him not to wander off.

The stranger smiled, and Debbie looked up at him. "I'm so sorry. He has a habit of going missing."

"No need to apologize," the man replied warmly. "We were discussing the harvest, and your curious boy here is concerned about the corn going missing."

Debbie was taken aback by Jared's sudden interest; he rarely engaged with strangers or showed much curiosity about farming. "It's not that kind of harvest, Jared. I told you that already."

Intrigued by this captivating stranger, Debbie watched as he effortlessly connected with her son. Gabe turned to Jared with a playful grin, acknowledging his curiosity. "Your mama has been teaching you about the harvest, has she?"

Jared nodded eagerly. "*Mamm* says it's essential to learn about God's gifts. Is the harvest one of God's gifts?"

"Absolutely," Gabe affirmed, sharing a knowing look with Debbie. "Your mother is a wise woman."

"Thank you," Debbie murmured gratefully. "Well, we should head back now. You have to eat something, Jared."

"I had a little snack," Jared chimed in.

Debbie glanced at the man with a friendly smile. "I'm Debbie."

"Hi, I'm Gabe," he replied warmly.

"Are you visiting?" Debbie inquired.

"Yes, I'm Jed's brother," Gabe explained.

CHAPTER 18

*D*ebbie pondered Gabe's response for a moment, realizing that he must be related to Malachi as well. "Do you have a large family?"

Gabe chuckled warmly. "Not really. Not compared to some. I'm one of Jed's older brothers," he confessed. "You've met Malachi, right? Cherish's husband?"

"Yes," Debbie nodded. "Until we met Jed, we hadn't met any of Malachi's relatives at all. We really knew nothing."

"Malachi's the mystery, even to us," Gabe revealed, his gaze drifting into the distance. "When he chose *rumspringa,* he decided not to return to our family. Instead, he went straight to our uncle's community and stayed there. We lost contact with him. But we heard he got married."

"He did. Cherish is a wonderful young woman. Your whole family would adore her," Debbie murmured wistfully, a touch of sadness in her voice as she longed for the connection she once had with her own parents.

"I hope to meet her one day. It sounds like Malachi made a good choice for a wife."

Debbie nodded, glancing at Jared, who had been absorbed in their conversation. "We're glad to have met you too, Gabe," she said warmly.

"Are you related to Cherish?" he asked.

"By marriage. Her mother married my uncle. I came to live here on this orchard years ago."

"Well, it's wonderful to meet you and Jared."

Debbie knew she had to get away from this man who was so easy to talk with. She was marrying Fritz, so she couldn't and shouldn't be enjoying talking to this man. Just as she was about to move away, Jared suddenly ran off when another boy called him over. Gabe leaned against a massive oak tree, his eyes never leaving Debbie's as he asked gently, "What about Jared's father? Is he here tonight?"

Debbie looked down, her hands fidgeting with the hem of her apron. "He... he passed away before Jared was born," she admitted softly, her heart aching at the memory of her unfortunate past.

"I'm sorry to hear that. It must be so hard for you," Gabe murmured, genuine sympathy in his eyes.

"It is sometimes."

"I've heard Wilma takes care of others like they're her own family."

"She does." Debbie glanced around looking for Jared. "Oh no, where did he go this time?"

Gabe chuckled. "Don't worry, he can't have gone too far. Look. He's playing with those boys."

Debbie put a hand over her heart and breathed out. "Jared's not like other children, Gabe. He doesn't understand things the way they do."

"Every child is different. That's what makes them special."

Debbie couldn't explain the weight of responsibility heavy on her shoulders. She so often wondered why her son wasn't normal like the other children. The doctor had said there was nothing to worry about, but that still didn't change the fact that Debbie saw that he *was* different. Debbie wasn't sure if that was a good thing.

"Have you eaten anything yet?" she asked.

He shook his head. "I'm not really hungry. I traveled many hours today and all I did on the Greyhound was eat."

"I see. Does Jed know you're here?"

"I think he does. I'm just waiting for him to come to me. Don't let me stop you from eating. You don't have to stay here and talk with me."

Debbie smiled. "I don't mind staying here with you, Gabe. It's nice to have someone to talk to. Besides, I haven't eaten either."

"Then why don't we grab a bite together? I could manage a little," Gabe suggested.

She hesitated for a moment and then agreed.

As they walked to the food, Debbie couldn't help but steal glances at Gabe. His presence was calm and reassuring, making her feel safe.

As they ate, they talked about their lives and shared stories of their childhood. Gabe listened intently to every word Debbie said, his eyes never leaving hers.

He shrugged his shoulders. "My life isn't as interesting as yours. With my folks getting older, I've had to take over a lot of the farm's responsibilities. It doesn't give me much time to do much else."

"How did you get away to come here?" Debbie asked.

"I snuck away while my dad was taking a nap." He laughed and then Debbie realized he was joking, and she laughed too. "No, my brothers are there. They all wanted me to find Jed and bring him home."

"The prodigal son, is he?"

Gabe grinned. "Maybe. Yes, most likely. More than anything, we just want to know what he's doing and when he'll be coming home."

"Where are you staying?" Debbie asked.

"My uncle arranged for me to stay with Bishop Paul. My uncle was the one who told me that my brother had come to this community, following a young woman."

Debbie laughed because it sounded a little scandalous, but it wasn't. "That would be Krystal."

"Yes, that's her name."

Debbie looked around for Jared and saw his young friend walking away with his parents to go home. There were no other children around, including Jared. "I can't see Jared again."

"He wouldn't have gone far, would he? Don't you and he live here?"

Debbie nodded. "Yes."

"He could be in the house."

"But with all these people here he wouldn't have gone back to the house."

"That doesn't make much sense."

"He's my son. I know what he'd do." Debbie knew she sounded abrupt, but she knew her son better than anyone. "He could end up anywhere." Debbie got to her feet. "Excuse me, I'll have to go look for him."

"I'll help."

"Thank you, Gabe. I appreciate your help. But you don't have to—"

"Of course, I'll help," Gabe cut in, his tone gentle yet firm. "We'll find him, don't you worry."

Debbie grabbed a flashlight that she saw under one of the tables and made her way into the darkness of the orchard.

"Jared!" she called out, her voice echoing through the rows of apple trees. "Come out now, please!"

"Maybe he's climbed up one of the trees," Gabe suggested, squinting at the branches above them. "He wouldn't be the first adventurous boy to do that."

"True, but..." Debbie hesitated, biting her lip as she

considered the possibility. "He's never done that before."

"First time for everything. Let's check anyway, just to be sure."

"No, I want to check around here before he gets any further away."

Gabe kept up with Debbie as she shone the flashlight between the trees.

"I'm sure you're worrying over nothing. It's dark out here. He'll come back."

Debbie continued walking and flashing her light around. "Do you have children, Gabe?"

"No. I'm not married."

"Then please keep your advice about parenting to yourself." Debbie felt a little guilty for snapping, but she was tired of people giving her unsolicited advice on raising her child.

CHAPTER 19

Hundreds of miles away at Favor's house, Favor and Cherish found a way to have their own celebration in honor of the Baker Apple Orchard's first day of harvest.

Emma and Annie were also there while Simon, Zeke, Gus, and Melvin labored outside, helping prepare yards for the alpacas.

Harriet had prepared a delectable apple pie that filled the room with its sweet aroma. Emma and Annie had thoughtfully brought apple-related treats to add to the delightful spread.

Just for the occasion, Emma had made Apple Cider Doughnuts, which were infused with the rich flavor of apple cider, coated in a delicate cinnamon-sugar dusting. Annie, with help from her award-winning cake designer mother, had made a cake in the shape of an apple.

Cherish looked around at the group of friends, her heart warmed by their companionship and the relationships she'd created.

"You know," Cherish began, savoring a bite of a doughnut, "I do miss the orchard. It's been a while since we were there, Favor. It's been longer for you."

Favor nodded in agreement, her eyes reflecting fond memories. "I miss it too. There's something special about the orchard during harvest season." She looked around at the others and told them, "There's so much excitement in the air." She didn't miss the hard work though, but she wasn't about to admit that in front of her mother-in-law. In the past, Harriet had accused her of being lazy.

Cherish smiled warmly at her sister, sharing the same sentiments. "I miss it every day," she said. "But having good friends makes up for it."

Not wanting to be left out, Harriet sighed. "I miss my home too. I miss the sheep, and just having a place that I can call my own."

"Don't worry, Ma. You'll soon have your own house again."

Harriet's gaze softened, her thoughts drifting back to the familiar warmth of her old home. "You know, back in our little house, we didn't have much in terms of material possessions, but it was filled with love and a sense of belonging," she reminisced. "We had a little garden where I grew herbs and flowers, and a cozy fireplace that kept us warm during the colder months. It may not have been grand, but it was home."

"It was a nice house, Ma," Favor said.

Cherish leaned in. "I'd love to hear more about your life there."

A tender smile touched Harriet's lips. "Oh, there are so many stories. We worked hard, taking care of the sheep. It wasn't always easy, but we found joy in simple things. In the evenings, we'd gather around the fireplace, sharing stories and laughter. Those were the moments that made life truly rich. Then Favor came to live with us, giving us more things to talk about."

"Ma, I might never have said this, but I've always admired the dedication you and Melvin put into everything you do. Your home always felt warm and welcoming."

"Thank you, Favor," Harriet said looking around at the young women. "I do think it's essential to create a place where family and friends feel welcome. A home is more than just walls and a roof. It's the heart that resides within."

Emma chimed in, "You have a way of making people feel welcome, Harriet. It's a rare gift."

Harriet's cheeks flushed with modesty. "I just try to be there for my loved ones, guiding them when needed and offering a listening ear."

"I'm so thankful for all of you," Favor said, her voice filled with sincerity. "Each one of you has become family to me in a short time, and I can't imagine life without you."

Emma and Annie nodded in agreement; their friendship strengthened by the shared experiences they had been through. "We'll always be here for one another, through the highs and the lows," Annie assured.

Harriet beamed at the younger women, feeling a sense of responsibility and love toward them. "You young ones are like the branches of a tree, each unique but interconnected, supporting each other through every season of life."

Cherish wanted to burst out laughing at Harriet's comment, but she managed to control herself. Harriet was becoming less domineering. It seemed she acknowledged that this was Favor's home and not hers.

As they continued their conversation, Emma kept looking at Favor.

"Favor, you're not eating much," Emma pointed out gently, concern in her eyes. "Is something bothering you?"

Harriet, ever the caring mother-in-law, joined the conversation. "Favor's okay, aren't you?"

Favor gave Emma a reassuring smile. "I'm alright, really. Just not as hungry as I thought, I suppose."

"Hmm. I know how both you and Cherish like sweet treats." Emma looked at her intently, a glimmer of understanding in her eyes. "Favor, are you... are you expecting?" she asked softly.

Favor's gaze shifted to Cherish, who shrugged her shoulders with a teasing smile, leaving the decision to Favor.

With a deep breath, Favor decided it was time to share her secret with her closest friends. "Yes," she admitted, her voice barely above a whisper. "I am pregnant."

Annie's eyes widened in surprise and delight. "Oh, Favor, that's wonderful news!"

Emma beamed at her friend, reaching out to hold Favor's hand. "Congratulations. I'm so happy for you."

Favor chuckled softly at their excitement. "Thank you all, but could we keep this news between us for a while? I want to wait a bit longer before sharing it with the whole entire world."

Emma and Annie nodded, understanding the significance of the request. "Of course, Favor," Emma said. "We'll keep your secret safe."

"Which one of us will be next?" Cherish asked, looking around.

"I know it won't be me," Harriet said with a laugh.

Cherish laughed, playfully elbowing Harriet. "Oh, come on, Harriet. You never know what the future holds. Maybe one day, you'll be surprised."

Harriet chuckled and shook her head. "I highly doubt that, but I'll keep an open mind."

Emma's eyes sparkled mischievously. "You never know, Harriet. Stranger things have happened!"

Annie joined in the banter, teasing Harriet as well.

"Yeah, you might find yourself falling for some dashing Amish gentleman out there."

Cherish was shocked and a hush fell over the room. "Harriet is married to Melvin."

Annie clapped a hand over her mouth. "Oh my. I'm so sorry. I knew that, but I temporarily forgot."

Harriet blushed slightly, trying to hide her amusement. "Alright, alright, enough jokes," she said, trying to change the topic. "Let's get back to talking about Favor. We should plan another small gathering to celebrate the good news. How about this time next week?"

As the others agreed, Cherish sat staring at Harriet. She thought they had a friend group of four. Did they now have a friend group of five? Was she going to be there all the time? It wouldn't be the same.

Favor looked touched by their enthusiasm. "You don't have to go through all that trouble."

"Nonsense," Annie insisted. "This is big news, and we need to celebrate properly. Besides, it's not every day we get to welcome a new little one into the community!"

Cherish smiled warmly at Favor. "They're right, you know. Let us do this for you. It'll be a wonderful way to share the joy with our closest friends."

Emma nodded in agreement. "Exactly! We'll make it a special and intimate gathering, just for us because we're still keeping it secret." Emma put her finger up to her mouth, acknowledging it was to be kept quiet.

Favor's heart swelled with gratitude. "Thank you, all

of you," she said, her voice choked with emotion. "I'm truly blessed to have friends like you. Well, a mother-in-law, a sister and two friends."

"We feel the same way about you, Favor. We're all family here," Annie said.

Favor wiped away a tear. "I don't know what I'd do without you all."

As if Harriet had read Cherish's earlier thoughts, she said, "Thank you all for accepting me as part of this wonderful circle. I've had more fun today than I have in some time."

Annie's cheeks flushed with embarrassment. "I'm really sorry for my momentary lapse there," she said, looking at Harriet apologetically. "I know you and Melvin are married. I had no idea why I said what I did. I really should think before I speak sometimes."

Harriet patted Annie's hand reassuringly. "No harm done, dear. It happens to the best of us. But let's focus on Favor and her happy news."

Favor put her hand on her stomach, which still looked quite flat. "This little one will be blessed to have such amazing aunties and an extraordinary grandmother."

Cherish playfully nudged Favor. "And let's not forget the uncles who are working so hard outside."

Favor chuckled. "Yes, of course. Malachi, Zeke, and Gus will be wonderful uncles too."

When there was a silent moment, Cherish said, "I wonder how everyone's getting along at the harvest."

"Getting along, or getting on?" Harriet asked with a smile hinting around her lips.

Cherish shrugged her shoulders. "I mean getting on, but... now that I think about it, I wonder how Krystal and Jed are doing."

"Jed is still there, so that's a good sign," Favor commented.

CHAPTER 20

*K*rystal noticed Jed was looking around and seemed distracted. It was unusual to see him so quiet. "Where's your brother?"

"I saw him walk down a row of trees with Debbie. They haven't come back yet. What's that about?"

Krystal sighed. "It can only mean one thing. Jared's gone missing again."

"I don't know why everyone worries so much about him. I used to disappear for hours when I was a kid."

"She's overprotective. Let's go see if we can help look for him." Krystal got to her feet and pleaded with Jed to come with her. He finally relented.

They walked into the orchard until they saw Debbie's flashlight. Debbie and Gabe were on their way back. Jed grumbled, "I don't know what he's doing here, but now I'm about to find out. Hey, Gabe!"

"How are you, brother?" Gabe asked.

"Good, good," Jed said, swallowing hard. "What brings you here?"

Gabe hesitated for a moment, glancing around before leaning in closer. "Well, I wasn't planning on coming, but the family..." He trailed off, looking away, before meeting Jed's gaze once more. "The family sent me here to check up on you."

"Check up on me?" Jed repeated, his mind racing with questions. "I knew it."

Debbie stepped forward. "Excuse me. Jared's gone missing again. I'll keep looking."

"Did you look in the house?" Krystal asked.

"No. I didn't think he'd go there if everyone was out here. I'll check there." Debbie started striding to the house.

"I'll continue looking out here," Jed said.

"I'll come with you, Debbie." Krystal caught up with her, leaving Jed staring at his brother.

"Jed, you know as well as I do that you've always been independent," Gabe said gently. "But sometimes, that independence can lead to trouble. The family just wants to make sure you're okay."

"Okay? Of course, I'm okay! I'm building my own business, and I've got Krystal by my side. I don't need anyone checking up on me!"

"Was that Krystal with you just now?"

"Yes. I'll introduce you when she comes back."

"Jed, it's not just about you. It's about the family. We care about you, and we want to make sure you're not getting into something you won't be able to handle. We want you to be safe."

"Safe?" Jed scoffed, shaking his head. "I've been taking care of myself just fine, thank you very much. I've been doing that my whole life, so I don't know why everyone's suddenly so interested."

Gabe went to speak again, but Jed cut him off.

"Thanks for coming all this way, Gabe, but I don't need you or the family to look after me. I'm a grown man."

"Alright, Jed," Gabe said, raising his hands in surrender. "But just remember we're here for you if you ever need us."

"Sure. You're here, but you should be back at the farm where you belong," Jed muttered, turning away and walking back to the house. Jed then swung around to face his brother. "Where are you staying?"

"I'm staying with Bishop Paul."

This was bad. Jed felt like a child whose secrets had just been laid bare for all to see. He hoped the bishop hadn't revealed that Matthew had said he'd tried to run over him with a bus.

Wait, is that why Gabe was here?

Did Jed's family think he'd tried to kill someone?

Gabe added, "I don't plan to be here very long."

"You shouldn't have come," Jed grumbled as he stomped off to find Krystal.

CHAPTER 21

Wilma and Ada saw the exchange between Jed and Gabe.

"Jed seems to know that man," she observed, her voice barely above a whisper.

"I've noticed. When we find a moment, let's ask him who he is."

The remaining cookout attendees gradually dispersed, leaving behind only their footprints in the soft earth as evidence of their presence. Wilma and Ada exchanged a determined nod before making their way toward Jed, who was helping take plates to the house.

"Excuse me, Jed," Wilma began. "We couldn't help but notice you talking to this man as if you're close acquaintances. Do you care to introduce us?"

"It's nobody. Just my older brother, Gabe."

"Oh, how nice," Wilma almost squealed.

Ada heard and wasted no time rushing over to

Gabe, who was now talking with Samuel. "Welcome. It's a pleasure to meet another brother of Malachi and Jed. Wilma and I are good friends with both. Wilma is Malachi's mother-in-law." Ada looked over at Wilma and beckoned her over.

Gabe smiled at Wilma. "Hello, Wilma. I've heard a lot about you."

Wilma studied Gabe – he shared Jed's dark eyes, but there was something deeper, more contemplative, lurking behind them. She wondered what had brought him here.

"Your brother has been such a blessing to everyone. We've seen that in the short time we've known him," Wilma told Gabe sincerely. "He helped birth a cow, didn't he, Ada?"

"Sure did. That was at Malachi's farm and now he's making his home here."

"Oh, I didn't realize he was going to stay. Anyway, Jed always had a talent for lending a hand," Gabe agreed. "Family is important, and I guess that's why I'm here."

As they continued their conversation, Wilma saw what a nice young man he was. "Did you get something to eat?"

"I did thank you. I'm staying with your bishop, and I think I'm more tired than anything."

"We'd love it if you'd come back here for a meal one day before you go home," Wilma said.

He smiled broadly. "I'd love that." He looked over at

the house and he saw that Debbie had found Jared. "I best be going then."

"We'll see you at the Sunday meeting, will we?" Ada asked.

"Yes." He gave them both a nod and walked away.

"He seems nice," Wilma whispered to Ada.

"Yes, but I think that Jed's not too happy with him being here."

"Hmm, I thought the same. Let's see what he has to say, shall we?"

Ada nodded. "I'd love to find out more."

Samuel was standing there, barely saying a word.

"Well, what did you find out?" Ada asked him.

"Not much. We were just talking about farming. I knew he was staying with the bishop and that's all."

"See, Wilma? Just as well we came over. Samuel never gets much information."

Wilma nodded. "Let's find Jed and see what he has to say."

Jed was sitting down in the living room with Krystal when they found him. They sat down with them. "So, Gabe, your brother, is staying with the bishop then?"

"He is. I didn't know he was coming. It's a bit of a surprise. He's never left home before."

"Life can be full of surprises," Ada chimed in with a knowing smile.

"Thanks for pointing that out, Ada," Jed said with a

chuckle, shaking his head. "Sometimes it's hard to keep up with all the changes."

"Changes can be good, though," Wilma added thoughtfully. "They can bring us closer together."

"True," Jed agreed. "Or they can cause people to grow apart. Before I go tonight, I'll help with the cleaning up. I've noticed there is a lot."

Wilma's face lit up. "I won't say no to some extra hands."

They all got up and headed outside.

As they set about tidying the cookout area, Jed efficiently cleared away the remnants of food and collected trash. Wilma couldn't help but notice how effortlessly he worked.

With the cookout area finally cleared and organized, Jed wiped the sweat from his brow. "I'd best be getting back to Ada and Samuel's place," he announced, exhaustion creeping into his voice. "I appreciate you letting me stay with you while I get my bearings here in the community, Ada."

"We love having you there, Jed."

Jed headed back to the borrowed buggy, with Krystal walking with him so they could say goodbye alone.

Once Wilma and Ada were in the kitchen, Wilma's gaze lingered on the plate of leftover meat. "Red would've enjoyed that," she said softly, almost to herself, as if she could call him back with her words. Her eyes were tinged with sadness; she missed the stray who, within a few short days, had touched her heart.

"We'll find him, Wilma. We'll drive around the streets again tomorrow, *jah?*"

Wilma looked up at her friend and nodded, while sending up a silent prayer that somehow in some way Red would come back.

CHAPTER 22

*F*riday dawned bright and clear, a perfect day for a tour. Jed, with palpable excitement, hitched his newly refurbished wagon, its paint shining under the sun. Today marked a significant step in his new venture, and he wanted everything to go smoothly.

The tourists, an enthusiastic mix of couples and families, marveled at the gleaming wagon as they boarded from the designated pickup point. Exchanging pleasantries and discussing their expectations for the day, the mood was upbeat. With a gentle snap of the reins, Jed began the journey.

The scenic beauty of the Amish countryside left many tourists in awe. Verdant fields stretched out on both sides, dotted with farmhouses and barns, providing the perfect backdrop for Jed's stories and commentary about Amish life.

Everything went according to plan at all the stops along the way.

Upon reaching Baker Apple Orchard, however, the atmosphere shifted. As the wagon pulled in, the first face that greeted Jed was Matthew's.

Before Jed could introduce the orchard or its significance, Matthew was already bounding toward the wagon, a wide grin on his face.

"Welcome, everyone! I'm Matthew, and I'll be showing you around The Baker Apple Orchard today," he announced with enthusiasm.

Jed's brows furrowed, and he swiftly intervened, "Actually, Matthew, I've got it covered. You can go back to work. I hear you've got a lot of work to catch up with."

But it was as though Matthew hadn't heard him. The crowd was already following him into the orchard. With a practiced ease, he began pointing out the various apple varieties and sharing interesting snippets about the orchard's history.

The tourists, oblivious to the undercurrents of tension, were eager to learn and naturally gravitated to Matthew, who seemed to have a wealth of information and a newfound sense of confidence.

Jed watched, seething with suppressed anger. This was his tour, his business, and he had planned every detail meticulously. He hadn't expected to be sidelined in his own venture. It was simply unacceptable.

Jed leaned against the wagon and after a moment he

saw the funny side. He walked up and patted one of the two horses that pulled the wagon.

In taking over his tourists, Matthew was doing him a favor. He could have a rest while Matthew 'worked' for him and did it for free.

He wouldn't make a fuss, and neither would he bother Krystal with the information about what Matthew did. It was petty and childish.

As Matthew continued to guide the tourists around the orchard, Jed's mind began to wander. He wondered if he had made the right decision in starting this venture. Maybe he wasn't cut out for this kind of work. Perhaps he should have stuck to what he knew best, farming and tending to his animals.

But as he watched the tourists laughing and enjoying the beauty of the orchard, he realized that he had a passion for what he'd done today. Yes, there would be challenges along the way, but he wouldn't let one setback discourage him.

As Matthew finished up his tour and bid the tourists farewell, Jed suggested they visit the little shop on the orchard.

There, they could get apples and the produce that was created from the apples.

The tourists eagerly agreed, and Jed pointed them toward the little shop. Then he turned to Matthew, who had been silently observing the tourists, and extended his hand.

"Thank you, Matthew. You did a great job today," Jed said, smiling.

Matthew hesitated for a moment before shaking Jed's hand. "No problem, Jed. I just wanted them to get an accurate picture."

Jed gave him a smile and a nod then hurried to catch up with the group. He was pleased that he didn't have a heated exchange with Matthew. He was tempted, but being nice was worth it to see the shock on Matthew's face.

He overtook the group and stood at the door while they walked into the shop.

Jed watched as they excitedly examined the different types of apple pies, jams, and ciders. He felt a sense of a job well done as he thought about the hard work he had put into creating this business.

As the tourists made their purchases, Jed couldn't help but feel grateful for their support. He knew that he had made the right decision in starting this venture, and he was determined to take it further.

Ada and Wilma kept smiling at him too, grateful for a few extra dollars before the day was out. It was a win for everyone all 'round. He couldn't wait to tell Krystal.

CHAPTER 23

ilma and Ada had driven around looking for Red for three consecutive days, but he was nowhere to be seen. When the day of the pie contest arrived, Wilma hoped it would help her stop worrying about Red, at least for a little while.

Daphne stood back and surveyed the bustling community hall, a satisfied smile playing on her lips.

The hall was adorned with colorful handmade quilts, lovingly draped over the walls by members of the community. Wooden tables lined the perimeter, showcasing an array of handcrafted goods being sold for charity: carefully whittled birdhouses, jars of home-made preserves, and intricately embroidered doilies.

"Great job on the publicity, Daphne," called out Martha, a trusted friend and fellow member of their tight-knit community. "You've brought everyone together for a wonderful cause."

"Thank you, Martha, but it wasn't just me. It was a group of us," replied Daphne modestly. "We couldn't have done it without all your help and support."

At the heart of the hall stood the main event, a long table filled with apple pies submitted for the contest.

"Ah, Bishop Paul has arrived," Daphne said as the respected man entered the hall.

He approached the pie table with quiet dignity, his strong sense of duty evident in every step. As one of three judges for the contest, he would play a crucial role in deciding the winner.

"Good afternoon, Bishop Paul," Daphne greeted him warmly as he joined her at the judges' table. "Are you ready for the difficult task ahead?"

"I am, Daphne, and I'm looking forward to it." His eyes twinkling with good humor.

The three judges took their seats, and then Ada got busy cutting three slices out of each pie to present to the judges, careful to keep their numbers with them. No one knew who baked the pies, except Susan Maine, who kept all the entry forms and substituted the numbers for the names.

"It is time for the moment you've all been waiting for! The pie contest shall now commence!" Samuel announced.

The warm scent of freshly baked pies filled the air, mingling with animated conversations as friends and family gathered within the community hall.

"Wilma," Christina called out, weaving through the

crowd with her twin daughters in tow. "Isn't this just wonderful?"

"It is," Wilma replied. "I'm so pleased to see everyone here."

"Me too. The girls have been looking forward to this," Christina said, gesturing toward her daughters who were excitedly chattering about their favorite kinds of pies.

"We helped *Mamm* make a cherry pie!" one of the twins exclaimed, bouncing on the balls of her feet. "But she said this wasn't a cherry pie contest so we have to eat it when we get home."

Wilma smiled at her. "Well, I'm sure it will taste great."

"I'm sure it will," Joy said as she joined them with her two daughters. "Your pies are amazing, Christina. Did you enter one today?"

"No, I didn't. Well, I did, but someone took a bite out of it, so it wasn't fit to enter."

"Mamm, are you all right?" Joy asked, noticing the distant look in her mother's eyes.

"Of course, dear," Wilma replied, snapping back to the present. "Just lost in thought for a moment."

"About Obadiah?" Christina ventured, a knowing look in her eyes.

Wilma's mouth fell open. What had Christina heard? "I'm not sure what you mean."

"You looked pretty friendly with him when I saw you both at the meeting."

Wilma nodded. "He's gone back home. He was a good friend. Still is, I suppose. Do you have a pie entered, Christina?"

"No. I think it's time to watch the judges taste the pies."

"Agreed," said Wilma as they made their way through the buzzing hall, their laughter and banter joining the chorus of voices that filled the space.

Wilma was delighted when she noticed Carter with young Iris, who clung to his hand like a lifeline. The little girl's face lit up at the sight of the baked delights on the table.

"Look at all the pies, Iris," Carter said, pointing to the pies.

"When can we taste them?" Iris squealed, her excitement contagious.

"Soon, I think."

Wilma waved to them and they waved back.

"Wilma, come this way," Ada called out, beckoning her friend over.

The judges began sampling the various pies. Murmurs and whispers filled the air as onlookers speculated about the judges' expressions as they tasted the samples.

"Which pie did you make, Wilma?" Ada asked.

"I saw Susan put number four on mine," Wilma whispered. "But it's not about winning – it's about participating and supporting our community."

"Of course," Ada agreed with a laugh. "But you're still wanting to win, right?"

Wilma stifled a giggle. "Right."

As the judges finished sampling the last of the pies, a hush swept over the room. The judges compared notes and after a few minutes, the bishop stood up and cleared his throat, commanding the attention of all present.

"Thank you to everyone who participated in the pie contest," he began, his voice strong and steady. "It was a difficult decision, but after much deliberation, we have unanimously chosen pie number six as the winner."

A collective gasp followed by applause filled the hall. Wilma couldn't help but feel a twinge of disappointment, quickly overshadowed by curiosity.

"What's your number, Ada?"

"Not number six," Ada whispered back.

The bishop continued, "We found the apple to have just the correct amount of spice and moistness and the pastry was just right."

"Who made the delicious pie?" Ada wondered aloud, echoing the thoughts of many gathered in the crowded room.

Wilma couldn't deny her own curiosity, watching as the crowd buzzed with excitement and speculation.

Susan furrowed her brow as she scanned the list of names, searching for the mysterious baker behind pie number six. The room buzzed with anticipation while people nudged each other, whispering their guesses and theories. Wilma's heart raced as she found herself caught up in the mystery.

"Well, Susan?" the bishop asked. "Who baked number six?"

Everyone looked at Susan and she became even more flustered, dropping her notes all over the floor. "Oh, dear. Sorry," she announced to everyone. She stooped down and picked them up. Once she found the correct page, she looked up at the crowd. "It says here, anonymous."

"Anonymous?" the bishop asked as he looked over the crowd. "Who entered as anonymous? That wasn't an option."

CHAPTER 24

*E*veryone looked around the crowd, expecting someone to come forward to claim that they were the winning baker.

Instead, a hush filled the room.

Ada blinked, her round face reflecting the same curiosity as the crowd. "How could you let someone enter without getting a name, Susan? You had one job to do."

Wilma watched as Susan shifted uncomfortably, clearly flustered by the unexpected turn of events. "Well," she began, hesitating for a moment, "the pie was just... there. Left with the others, along with a note."

Ada stepped forward. "Show me that note." As Susan handed it over, Ada's eyes quickly scanned the shaky writing. "The note also says, 'Enjoy this humble offering from an old hand.' How peculiar!"

"An old hand?" Christina mused, rubbing her chin

thoughtfully. "Perhaps it's a long-lost recipe from someone who used to participate in contests years ago? Or maybe it's someone who's too shy to reveal themselves."

"Or it could be someone trying to stir up some excitement," Joy added.

"It hardly seems fair to the other entrants if the winner isn't here to claim her prize," Daphne added.

As whispers and speculation continued to fill the air, Wilma couldn't help but be intrigued by the anonymous baker. She tried to think of anyone within their community who would have reason to hide their identity, but no woman came to mind. "Why would someone go through all the trouble of crafting such a delicious pie, only to remain hidden in the shadows?"

"Regardless of who made it," Ada said, "they deserve our congratulations. That pie must've been something else for all three judges to vote for it."

Joy suggested, "Some people don't need recognition or praise; they just enjoy making others happy."

"Whoever they are," Christina chimed in, her voice full of admiration, "they've certainly brought some excitement to the contest."

Wilma smiled, nodding in agreement. And as the crowd continued to murmur and guess, she couldn't help but feel a renewed sense of unity within their community—all because of one mysterious, anonymous pie baker.

The bishop walked to the middle of the room.

"Come now, don't be shy. If the baker of pie six is here, who wrote down their name as anonymous, please make yourself known."

Wilma watched as the room grew quiet again, the anticipation hanging heavy in the air. The gentle tapping of her foot echoed against the wooden floorboards.

Suddenly, a figure emerged from the crowd and walked toward the bishop—a familiar face with a hesitant smile.

"Uh...excuse me," Eli stammered, his hands clasped together nervously. "I know who baked the pie."

A collective gasp filled the room as everyone stared at him, their eyes widening with shock and disbelief.

"Okay, Eli. Who baked the pie?" the bishop asked.

The corners of Eli's lips tilted upward. "I did it."

Ada frowned and looked at Susan, who returned her frown. "You?" Ada inquired. "But how…"

"Yes," he replied, his voice firm despite the trembling of his hands. "I know it's unusual for a man to enter a pie contest, but I assure you, it was I."

"Unusual is an understatement," Joy chimed in, crossing her arms as she studied Eli's earnest expression. "Why didn't you put your name on it, then?"

"Because..." Eli hesitated, casting a glance at Wilma before lowering his gaze back to the floor. "I wasn't sure if it was good enough to enter. I just followed Frannie's recipe. Her pies were the best I ever tasted."

Wilma's eyebrows knitted together as she considered his words. She knew how much Eli missed his late wife, and she found herself touched by his desire to honor her memory in such a personal way. She could only imagine the courage it took for him to stand there and lay claim to the creation.

"Are you certain, Eli?" Susan asked gently, her eyes softening with empathy. "We don't want you to feel pressured into taking credit if it wasn't really you."

"*Jah,* I'm sure."

"Alright, then," the bishop declared, breaking through the quiet. "Congratulations, Eli. It was a truly delicious pie." He then filled out the winner's certificate and presented it to Eli.

Eli looked down at it and smiled.

"Now everyone can taste the leftover pies, can't they?" the bishop asked Susan.

"Yes. We have plates and cutlery, enough for all."

"Thank you," Eli replied, holding up his certificate.

The room erupted into applause.

As Wilma clapped along, her eyes fixed on Eli as he braced himself for the barrage of questions that were surely to follow.

Ada was the first to gravitate to Eli and ask a question. "How did you come to make such a wonderful pie? We know you live on your own. Do you bake a lot?"

Eli hesitated for a moment, then inhaled deeply before answering. "Well, I used to watch my wife bake."

"Really?" Joy chimed in, her eyes wide with surprise. "We never knew you had such talent hidden away!"

"I didn't think it was right to let her skills go to waste after she passed. I decided to give it a try."

Wilma knew exactly how he felt. It was his way of keeping something of his wife alive.

The room swelled with warmth and admiration, as if everyone was touched by him baking his wife's pie recipe. The moment served as a reminder that even amidst sorrow, there was space for a touch of happiness, even if it came in the form of fond memories from days gone by.

CHAPTER 25

*E*li's smile was a brilliant beacon of light as he stared at the certificate, his eyes tracing the elegant calligraphy that declared him the winner.

"Look at him." Joy leaned in, her voice low as she spoke to Wilma. "Isn't that so sweet?"

Wilma nodded, her own emotions welling up inside her. "It's beautiful to see."

"Can you imagine the love he must've had for her, to learn her pie recipe and make it so perfectly?" Christina added, her eyes shimmering with unshed tears. "I hope Mark will feel like that for me if I go home to *Gott* first."

"Wilma," Carter called out, his voice cutting through her thoughts. "Iris wants to know if there's any of Eli's pie left."

"Tell her I'll fetch her a slice," Wilma replied,

grateful for the excuse to step away from the emotional whirlwind surrounding her.

As she made her way toward the table laden with pies, she couldn't help but steal one more glance at Eli. He stood tall, his shoulders squared, and his chin lifted.

"Here you go, Iris," she said, handing the young girl a generous slice of pie. "Savor it slowly because this is a recipe that was made with love."

"Thank you, Grandma!" Iris beamed, her eyes wide with delight.

As Iris dug into her pie, Wilma allowed herself a small, contented smile. It seemed that sometimes, love could be found in the most unexpected places - like the tender crumb and sweet aroma of a perfectly baked apple pie. "I'm so happy you came, Carter."

"The community was a big part of Florence's life. I thought it wouldn't hurt for Iris to come to a few things like this. It will broaden her horizons. That'll form part of her education about different lifestyles and different choices."

Wilma smiled but didn't really understand what they were trying to do with Iris's upbringing and education. She still couldn't get past the fact that they'd allowed Iris to name her baby brother. "While you're here, I might find Debbie and tell her about the house."

"Sure thing. We can take her there tomorrow if you're both free?"

"That would be wonderful." Wilma's eyes scanned the

room as she searched for Debbie. She saw her holding Jared's hand as he looked at the pies with a gleam in his eye. It looked like he wanted to eat all of them. "Debbie."

Debbie looked up as Wilma walked over to see her. "Everyone's having a great time. This was such a good idea, Wilma."

"It was Ada's idea."

"I know."

"I do want to discuss something with you."

"What is it?" Debbie asked.

"It's about you and Fritz."

"Yes."

"Come," Wilma beckoned, leading Debbie to a corner of the room where they could talk freely. Jared came along with them. Wilma didn't want to talk in front of Jared, so she suggested that Jared go over to Iris. He quickly agreed.

"What is it, Wilma?"

"Debbie, I want to give you and Fritz a house," Wilma blurted out, unable to contain her excitement any longer. "It's really from Levi."

"But... why...?"

"I have these houses Levi left me, and you're his niece. I'll see that Bliss gets her fair share too, but I know Levi would want you to have one. He saw you as his daughter."

Debbie's mouth dropped open, her eyes brimming with astonishment. "A house? For us?" she stammered, her cheeks flushing pink. "Oh, Wilma, I don't know what to say. That's so... generous."

"Levi would've insisted," Wilma said, placing a comforting hand on Debbie's arm. "I'm just hoping Fritz will be okay with it."

"I don't see why he wouldn't. He'll be just as delighted as I am. This is just... so unexpected. I can hardly find words."

"Sometimes," Wilma whispered, her voice full of wisdom and experience, "the most unexpected gifts are the ones that bring us the greatest joy."

Debbie pulled Wilma into an embrace of gratitude before stepping back again. "Thank you," she said solemnly.

Wilma nodded and smiled reassuringly. "Carter can take us to view it tomorrow."

"That would be wonderful."

"I just hope it will be good enough."

"It will be. I don't mind what it's like, Wilma. It'll be such a good start for us."

Wilma smiled, but what she meant was she hoped it was good enough for Fritz.

CHAPTER 26

*A*fter Debbie was home from work the next afternoon, Carter's car pulled up in front of Wilma's house, the engine purring softly like a contented cat. His warm smile greeted them as they climbed into the vehicle, and Debbie couldn't help but feel a flutter of anticipation in her chest.

"Hello. Ready to see your new home, Debbie?" Carter asked.

"Definitely," Debbie replied.

"Can you tell Debbie what happened to the house regarding the damage?" Wilma asked.

Carter adjusted his sunglasses before answering. "Storm damage. But don't worry, everything's been repaired and updated. It's as good as new. Jared's not coming?"

"No. He's staying at home with Krystal. She's playing games with him." As they drove down the winding country road, Debbie couldn't help but imagine what her new life with Fritz would look like – the mornings spent baking bread in a cozy kitchen, the summer evenings spent rocking on the front porch beneath the stars. The winter evenings by a crackling fire sipping hot chocolate with marshmallows.

The car came to a gentle stop in front of a modest white house nestled among tall trees, their leaves creating a canopy of dappled sunlight. The sight stole Debbie's breath away, and she felt a lump form in her throat.

"Here we are," Carter announced. "Your new home."

"It's beautiful," Debbie said.

Debbie and Wilma stepped out of the car, their eyes wide as they took in the charming scene before them. The house had a welcoming air about it, with its neat flower beds and freshly painted shutters. It was the kind of place that seemed to promise love and laughter within its walls.

"Come on," Carter beckoned, leading them up the stone path to the front door. "Let me show you the inside."

As they stepped into the house, Debbie felt a surge of awe. The living room was well lit, with honey-colored hardwood floors and soft blue walls that seemed to whisper serenity.

"Through here," Carter guided them, "is the kitchen. It's been completely redone."

The kitchen gleamed with newness – white cabinets and an over large sink beneath a window over-looking the backyard. Debbie could almost smell the aroma of freshly baked bread and hear the sizzle of eggs frying on the stove.

"There are two bedrooms at the back of the house and a smaller one at the front."

"Will it be big enough?" Wilma asked.

"It will be plenty big," Debbie insisted, her excite-ment bubbling over. "I just can't wait to tell Fritz all about it. He won't be able to believe it."

"Are you certain he will approve of the house?" Wilma asked gently, placing a hand on Debbie's shoulder.

"Absolutely. This house is perfect for us. Thank you so much, Wilma." Debbie leaned forward and gave Wilma a hug.

"Then let's get you two lovebirds settled in!" Carter declared, his broad smile stretching from ear to ear.

"Our wedding is December third, so we'll move in then. Although, we will probably get it ready before then."

"It's here waiting," Wilma said.

Debbie couldn't help but grin as she imagined Fritz's reaction, his eyes widening in disbelief when they would walk through the front door together.

"And thank you, Carter for helping with this. This means more to me than words can say."

"No need to thank us, Debbie," Wilma responded, her own emotions shimmering in her eyes. "It's our pleasure to help you and Fritz begin your lives together."

As they made their way back to Carter's car, Debbie took one more walk around the outside of the house while Wilma and Carter headed to the car.

Carter opened the car door for Wilma. "Congratulations, Wilma."

Wilma hesitated before she climbed in. "What for?"

"For becoming a grandmother again… in the future, with Favor."

"Oh, I see. Florence told you?"

"I hope you don't mind. We don't keep secrets."

Wilma smiled. "I don't mind at all, but please don't tell anyone else."

As she got into the front seat, he shrugged his shoulders. "Who would I tell?"

Debbie headed to the car, elated. Everything was falling into place. The house was a gift that would change their lives forever.

She got into the backseat of the car. "I know Fritz will love this place. Tonight, I'm going to write to him and tell him all about it."

"Why not call him?" Carter asked.

"I only call in emergencies. He doesn't really like to talk on the phone, and I've got so much to say. It'll be better to write."

CHAPTER 27

That night after everyone was asleep, Debbie commenced her letter.

'Dearest Fritz,' she began, her hand trembling slightly. 'I have such wonderful news to share with you! Wilma has generously offered to give us a house. I still can't believe it, and my heart is full of gratitude. We now have somewhere we can live after we're married.'

Debbie paused, picturing Fritz's strong jawline and gentle eyes reacting to this news. She continued, 'There is so much happening in preparation for our wedding. Florence has offered to make the dresses, and she'll make suits for you as well unless you have organized something else. As you know, Wilma and Ada are excited about the food, and especially the cakes."

Jared appeared in Debbie's doorway. "What are you doing awake?"

"I can't sleep, Debbie." He walked over and quickly jumped under the covers with her.

"Excuse me? It's *Mamm,* not Debbie."

"But Debbie's your name."

"I know that, but you're my son so you'll call me *Mamm.*"

He shrugged. "Don't see why."

"Because that's just the way things are."

"So, what are you doing?" He looked down at her letter.

"I'm writing a letter to Fritz. When we get married, you'll call him *Dat.* Are you excited about that?"

Jared nodded, then he ran out of the room and came back with tiny folded pieces of paper. "Can you put these in the letter?"

"Of course. What are they?"

"Drawings. Can I tell Fritz something too?" Jared asked, his face lighting up with excitement.

"Of course. What would you like to tell him?"

"Tell Fritz about the harvest," Jared urged, his eagerness palpable. "And that there was no corn this year."

Debbie hesitated but decided to honor the boy's request. 'Jared wants you to know that there was no corn to be found,' she wrote, her script a bit more hesitant. She was grateful Fritz understood that Jared had his unique way of seeing the world.

"Thank you, *Mamm.*" Jared smiled up at her. "I wonder what he'll think about that."

"We'll soon find out. I'll mail this letter first thing tomorrow. Now, do you think you'll be able to sleep?"

"I dunno."

"Do you want me to tuck you in?"

"Nah, that's for babies." He got out of bed and walked out of the room.

Debbie smiled fondly at her son's retreating figure, finishing her letter to Fritz with a loving sign-off. 'I cannot wait for us to begin our life together, surrounded by our dear family and friends,' she penned. 'Until then, take care and know that my heart belongs to you. Forever yours, Debbie.'

Debbie carefully sealed the letter and placed it where she'd see it in the morning.

Minutes later, as she lay in bed, her mind wandered to the upcoming wedding. It seemed like just yesterday when she and Fritz had first met, and now they were about to embark on a new chapter of their lives together. She thought of the life they would build, the love they would share, and the family they would create.

Amidst her thoughts, the sound of soft footsteps approached her room. Jared peeked in, a sheepish smile on his face.

"Can't sleep, huh?" Debbie asked, patting the bed beside her.

Jared nodded, climbing under the covers. "I keep thinking about Fritz and the letter," he admitted.

Debbie wrapped her arm around her son, drawing

him close. "It's natural to be excited," she reassured him. "Fritz will be thrilled to hear from us, especially about the harvest."

"Yeah," Jared replied. "I hope he likes the pictures. It's of Favor's alpacas."

"I'm sure he'll love your pictures," Debbie said with a warm smile. "Your drawings are always wonderful."

Jared snuggled closer to his mother, his eyelids growing heavy. "Do you think he'll write back soon?"

"I hope so," Debbie replied softly. "But it might take some time, considering the distance."

Jared soon drifted off to sleep, his dreams filled with thoughts of his future 'Dat' and the adventures they would have together.

Debbie lay awake for a while longer, her heart full of love for her son and the man she would soon call her husband. She knew that their lives were about to change in the most beautiful way, and she was grateful for every future moment they would share.

With a contented sigh, she whispered, "Goodnight, my sweet boy," before finally succumbing to sleep herself, dreaming of a bright future.

CHAPTER 28

a few days later, Debbie had just arrived home when Krystal called her back to the barn, saying she had a phone call.

Debbie passed Krystal on the porch. "Is it Fritz?"

"Yes."

Debbie's heart leaped and she raced toward the barn. He would've gotten her letter by now and would've been thrilled about the house.

She entered the dimly lit barn. The musty smell of hay mixed with the scent of the horses stabled nearby.

She picked up the receiver and took a breath to calm herself. "Hi."

"Hello, Debbie. I got your letter."

"Isn't it great?"

"It was good of her to offer it, but I cannot accept it."

"Are we talking about the same thing... the house?"

"Yes."

"Why can't you accept it? It's from Wilma, but she told me it's really from Uncle Levi." Debbie was disappointed. She could tell from Fritz's voice that he'd made up his mind about this. Wilma would be so hurt if they rejected her kind offer, and she couldn't bear the thought of hurting her feelings. There was a pause at the other end of the line and Debbie held her breath, hoping he'd change his mind.

"I can provide for my family, Debbie. I don't need anyone else's help."

"Wilma isn't trying to undermine your ability to provide. She sees this as a gift from my uncle Levi, not a handout."

"I appreciate the sentiment, but I must stand by my decision. I've made up my mind."

Debbie bit her lip, searching for the right words to bridge the gap between Fritz's stubborn pride and Wilma's kind intentions. "What if Uncle Levi had left it to me in his will? Wilma said he would've, but he knew Wilma would know what to do with what he left. She's simply doing what he would've done. That's how she explained it to me."

"I won't change my mind."

"Can you at least talk to Wilma?" Debbie pleaded. "Please, just listen to what she has to say."

"Alright, I'll speak with her and tell her what I've decided."

Debbie didn't know what to say.

She looked down at her hands, twisting her apron nervously. She understood Fritz's feelings, but she also knew how much Wilma wanted to help them. Her thoughts raced, trying to find a solution that would satisfy everyone.

"Maybe there's a way," she began hesitantly, "to let Wilma feel like she's helping without accepting the house outright?"

"How do you propose we do that?" Fritz asked.

She thought for a moment before answering. "What if, instead of taking the house as a gift, we agree to some sort of arrangement? Like... paying her back over time? That way, you're still providing for us, but we don't hurt Wilma's feelings by rejecting her generosity."

"What is the house like? I've had a look at some places that were for sale, but I couldn't have lived in any of them."

Debbie was worried about his high expectations. "It is small."

"How small?"

"I was so excited when I was there, and I can't remember if it had two bedrooms or three."

"There's a big difference between two and three. That's something you should've remembered. It sounds like it's too small for us and Jared. I should see it first before anything is discussed."

Then Debbie started worrying about Carter who was getting the transfer of ownership underway with his lawyer. All she could do was hope and pray that it would work out for the best. "Thank you for being willing to compromise. I know this isn't easy for you."

"I'm willing to look at all options for our family's sake," Fritz replied.

Debbie could hear the reluctance in his voice. "I know this situation puts you in a tough spot, Fritz. But please remember that Wilma's heart is in the right place. She genuinely wants to help."

There was a soft sigh from the other end of the line. "I do understand that. I just want our family to stand on its own feet and not be reliant on handouts."

"It's not a handout if we come up with an arrangement," Debbie said gently. "Think of it as a gesture of love and goodwill from someone who cares deeply about our well-being. If Uncle Levi truly intended for me to have the house, then it's not charity. It's family."

Fritz was silent for a few moments. "I don't know, Debbie. Let's discuss it further when I see the house."

"That sounds fair." She worried about what she'd say to Wilma.

"I have to go now. You've just given me something else to think about."

"What do you mean?" Debbie asked.

He hesitated as though he was choosing his words carefully. "How can I give you an answer when I haven't seen this place?"

"Isn't it enough that I like it?" she asked.

He gave a grunt. "You might like anything. I must go now. I've got lots to do."

"Bye."

"Goodbye, Debbie."

After hanging up the receiver, Debbie leaned against the barn wall, closing her eyes and taking a deep breath. She hoped that when Fritz saw the house and spoke to Wilma, he would see things from a different perspective. But for now, all she could do was wait.

Before Debbie could fully digest their conversation, the barn phone rang again, its jangling tone startling her. She picked it up apprehensively. "Hello?"

"It's me again," came Fritz's voice again, softer this time. "I've been thinking. I won't have time to see the house before the wedding, but... I've thought of a way we can make this work."

Debbie's heart swelled with hope. "Go on."

"If Wilma would be willing to accept payment for the house, maybe we could think of it as... buying it from her rather than her giving it to us. That way, I'd still feel like I'm doing my part to provide for our family."

Debbie's heart rate quickened, sensing a breakthrough. It was odd that he suggested that, but now he thought it was his idea. She didn't want to upset him, so she kept quiet. "I think Wilma might be open to that. It's a good compromise."

"I won't be able to discuss it with her before the wedding," Fritz admitted, a hint of regret in his voice.

"But could you talk to her about it on my behalf and see if she'd be open to the idea?"

Debbie hesitated for a moment. "I can talk to Wilma, but you're sure about this?"

There was a pause on the other end. "Yes," Fritz finally said. "It's a solution that might work for everyone."

Debbie took a deep breath. "I'll talk to her and see what we can arrange."

"Thank you, Debbie," Fritz said. "I know this isn't easy, but I trust you to handle it. When you're my wife, you'll have to get used to handling responsibility."

Debbie was taken aback. Wasn't raising a child by herself responsibility? What about her tea business that was growing every week? Fritz talked to her like she was an eighteen-year-old girl. If he was in front of her, she would've said something, but with him being so far away, she let it go.

"Are you still there, Debbie?"

"I am."

"I'll call you in a couple of days to see how you got on. Bye for now."

She heard the phone click in her ear.

As she hung up, a mixture of emotions swirled inside her. The hope of settling into a new home mingled with the stress of Fritz's expectations. Could she bridge the gap between Fritz's pride and Wilma's generosity?

IT WAS a rare night that Ada and Samuel weren't at Wilma's house. Wilma's kitchen was filled with the comforting aroma of a stew bubbling on the stove, a sign of an evening meal in the making. The homely scent combined with the familiar clatter of pots and pans created a backdrop of warmth as Debbie and Wilma worked side by side.

Wilma chopped fresh vegetables, her hands moving expertly, while Debbie stirred the stew, her thoughts preoccupied. Taking a deep breath, she ventured, "Wilma, there's something I need to discuss with you about the house."

Wilma looked up from her cutting board, her expression curious. "What is it, dear?"

Debbie took another deep breath, "Fritz called about the house. He got my letter telling him all about it. He has a request."

Wilma paused, her knife still, waiting for Debbie to continue.

"He was hoping, instead of accepting the house as a gift, that we could pay you back over time. He feels it would allow him to retain some pride in providing for our family." Debbie said, watching Wilma's face carefully for her reaction.

Wilma set the knife down and thought for a moment. The sizzle of onions being added to a pan was the only sound between them. "You mean, like a payback, like a loan?"

Debbie nodded, "Something like that. Would you be open to the idea?"

Wilma took a moment, then resumed chopping. "I offered the house because I wanted to help, not because I want payment. But I understand Fritz's perspective. It's important for a man to feel he's doing his part."

Debbie felt a surge of relief. "So, you'd be okay with it?"

Wilma smiled gently. "If it means you two can start your life together in a place you both feel comfortable, then yes. We can work out the details later. What's important is that you both are happy."

Debbie's eyes welled up with gratitude. "Thank you, Wilma. This means so much to both of us."

Wilma went back to her cutting. It didn't sit right with her. She wanted to give them a gift, but she hoped a face-to-face talk with Fritz would cause him to change his mind. Debbie seemed so wound up and stressed about it that Wilma thought it best to simply agree. That would ease Debbie's mind for the moment.

CHAPTER 29

Wilma sat in her living room, writing down a list of things such as wool, that she wanted to buy to make Favor's baby some knitted items.

She enjoyed the rhythmic sound of the rain against the windowpane, accompanied by the occasional giggles and chatter of Jared playing in the nearby room.

The tranquility of the scene was suddenly interrupted when Wilma noticed the silence from Jared's direction. Glancing up from her notebook, she peeked out the window and was taken aback to see Jared standing amidst the downpour.

With arms outspread, Jared's little face tilted up to catch every droplet, immersed in the beauty of nature.

"Jared!" Wilma called out, her voice a mix of astonishment and concern. Setting her embroidery aside, she hastened to the door. "Jared, come back in."

Jared's rain-soaked face lit up with delight when he saw her. "Aunt Wilma! The rain feels like tiny kisses from the sky."

With a chuckle, masked by her maternal concern, Wilma replied, "And those tiny kisses will give you a big cold if you stay out any longer."

"But Aunt Wilma," Jared began with a twinkle in his eye, "I wanted to see where the birds go when it rains."

Taking his hand, Wilma led him back inside, shaking her head in amused exasperation. "You and your endless curiosity. Come, let's dry you off, and then we can talk about those birds."

"Okay then," Jared murmured, his adventurous spirit momentarily subdued as he trailed behind her into the sanctuary of the house.

Once inside, Wilma gazed affectionately at him, amused by the boy's zest for life that sometimes drove him to the most unexpected places, like today's dance in the rain. His spark was a constant source of joy for her.

"Come on, let's get you warmed up," she suggested, leading him closer to the gentle glow of the fireplace. "How about some hot cocoa afterward?"

Jared's face brightened instantly at the thought. "Really? With marshmallows?"

"Of course," Wilma replied with a chuckle, noting how easily his spirits lifted.

She wrapped him in a towel and then sent him to

his bedroom to change into dry clothes. Then she set about making their hot drinks.

When he came back in, she knew she had to warn him about playing in the rain.

"You were all wet and if you get wet, you can get cold and then you might catch a cold or something even worse."

"I guess I didn't think that part through."

"Remember, Jared," she said, her voice low and full of love, "there is a time for adventure and a time for caution. And sometimes, we need to be reminded of which is which."

"I'll be more careful next time, but I still like the rain."

"I like it too, but it's so much nicer to watch the rain than to actually be in it, wouldn't you say?"

He shrugged his shoulders. "I like to be in it."

Wilma gave up. She'd tried her best.

THE RAIN CONTINUED its steady rhythm outside, wrapping the house in a soothing blanket of sound. Wilma glanced at Jared, who sat near the fireplace, his damp clothes replaced by warm, dry ones. The firelight danced on his face, illuminating his curious eyes as they darted around the room.

Wilma wanted to understand Jared better, so she

took the opportunity of them being alone together. Perhaps he'd open up to her.

"Jared," Wilma said softly, drawing his attention back to her. "What were you thinking, standing out there in the rain like that?"

"Sorry, Aunt Wilma," he replied sheepishly. "I just... I don't know. It felt important."

"Important?" She raised an eyebrow, intrigued by his response. "Why is that?"

He hesitated, searching for the right words. "It's just... I've always wondered where the birds go when it rains. And today, I thought maybe if I stood out there long enough, I might find out."

Wilma couldn't help but smile at his earnestness. "Ah, I see. Your curiosity got the better of you, then?"

"I guess so," he admitted, looking down at his hands.

"Curiosity is a wonderful thing, Jared, but we must also remember to take care of ourselves."

"*Jah,*" he agreed, his gaze meeting hers with sincerity.

"Alright, then." She leaned back in her chair and took a deep breath, enjoying the warmth of the fire and the comforting scent of the burning wood. "So, let's talk about your question. Where do you think the birds go when it rains?"

Jared's eyes lit up with excitement, thrilled that she was engaging with him on this topic. "Well, I thought maybe they hid under leaves or in small holes in trees. Or maybe they fly away to somewhere dry. I know if it's raining here, it might not be raining a few miles away."

"Those are good theories," Wilma acknowledged, her mind replaying memories of her own childhood when she used to ponder such questions. "I think many birds do find shelter in trees or other places that protect them from the rain."

"Really?" Jared's eyes widened with wonder. "I thought they could've just disappeared."

"No, they don't just disappear." Wilma chuckled. "They're clever creatures, able to do what they need to do to survive."

"But do you know where they go?" Jared asked again, his eyes wide and curious.

Wilma gazed out the window at the gray sky, raindrops gently tapping on the tin roof of the porch. "Perhaps," she mused, "they find shelter underneath the leaves of trees or inside small holes in the tree trunks. They find shelter like we do. We go into our houses. We don't stand out in the middle of the driveway spinning in a circle."

Jared laughed.

Wilma wondered how she could divert his attention from the birds. She knew Jared often helped Ada in the kitchen, but she wasn't there today.

"Would you like to help me peel apples for tonight's pie?"

"Can I?"

"You sure can."

"Can we do it now?"

Wilma chuckled again. "How about we enjoy a rest first."

His mouth turned down at the corners.

"Okay. Let's make a start and get those apples peeled."

He got up and ran to the kitchen and pulled the bucket of apples out of the cupboard.

Wilma helped him lift the bucket onto the table. "Now, you pick out about twelve of the nicest apples for the pie."

"Really? I thought the nice ones were used for candy apples and the damaged ones were used for pies."

"Maybe, but today we're going to use the good ones."

He chose the apples and set them in a row.

Ada had already shown him how to peel off the skin with a special peeler rather than a knife. His nimble fingers worked quickly and efficiently.

"Remember, Jared, slow and steady wins the race," Wilma cautioned, chuckling at his eagerness.

He looked up at her and grinned.

As they worked side by side, Wilma couldn't help but feel grateful for these simple moments together. "Jared," she said suddenly, struck by an idea, "what if we build a little birdhouse together? That way, the birds will have a place to go when it rains."

"Can we?" Jared's face lit up with excitement.

"Of course," she confirmed, warmth filling her heart as she saw the joy in his eyes. "We'll work on it together, as a team."

"I can't wait to start."

"Let's finish these apples first," Wilma said.

Wilma didn't know the first thing about making anything except food. Her mind drifted to Obadiah. Having a man around would sure have come in handy.

CHAPTER 30

$\mathcal{I}$n Wilma's kitchen, the aroma of a pot pie filled the air as Ada and Wilma bustled about, preparing the evening meal. The setting sun cast a golden glow through the window, creating a cozy atmosphere as the two friends worked side by side, sharing quiet conversations sprinkled with a little community gossip.

Ada paused for a moment, her eyes resting on Wilma, who seemed lost in thought. "What's on your mind, Wilma?" she gently inquired.

Wilma sighed. "It's Favor. I mean, I'm not there to help her. Would she want me there for the birth? She hasn't said one thing about that."

With a sympathetic smile, Ada set down her wooden spoon and turned to face her friend. "That's months away. Let's give her some time. She wouldn't have thought that far yet," she reassured.

"I know, Ada, but I do want to be there to share in the excitement. I hear their house is small, so they might not have room for me."

"Not a problem. Stay at Cherish's house for the birth."

Just then, they heard the soft patter of footsteps approaching the kitchen. "What are you two whispering about? Is there something going on? I heard someone say birth. Who's pregnant?"

Both women exchanged a hesitant glance, unsure whether to share the news. But Krystal was like family, so it wouldn't matter if she knew. "Have a seat," Wilma said.

Krystal settled at the kitchen table, her gaze fixed on Ada and Wilma, waiting for them to speak. "It's Favor, isn't it? What's happening? Or is it Cherish, or someone else?" she asked, sensing that something significant was being kept from her.

Wilma took a deep breath. "Favor has some happy news, but she wanted to wait until she's over the three-month mark before telling anyone."

Krystal's face lit up. "I'm so happy for her. I won't say a word."

"A word about what?" Debbie asked as she entered the kitchen.

Of course they couldn't tell Krystal and not tell Debbie. Everyone looked at Wilma, waiting for her to speak. "Favor is having a baby."

Debbie squealed. "Oh, I can't wait to visit them.

They're going to get alpacas too. When is the baby due?"

Wilma and Ada looked at one another, and Ada counted the months on her fingers. "Maybe March next year."

"That's not that far away."

Just then, Jared ran into the kitchen. "Favor's having a baby? How did that happen?"

The women exchanged amused glances, and Wilma couldn't help but chuckle softly. "Oh, my dear boy," she said, pulling him into an embrace, "that's a story for another time. "But it is a secret for now, Jared."

Debbie added, "That's right and we can't tell anyone for the moment."

Jared nodded. "I won't tell anyone."

"Good boy," Ada said.

"But can I tell them about the alpacas?"

Ada laughed. "Do you even know what they are?"

"I learned about them in school."

On Sunday, laughter and conversation of community members filled the air as they gathered around the long wooden tables laden with food.

"Isn't all this just lovely?" Ada asked as she ladled out generous helpings of chicken wings onto her plate.

Wilma agreed, "Yes, and it's always wonderful to see everyone together like this."

After they sat down, Wilma couldn't help but notice her friend's furrowed brow. "What's troubling you?"

"It's Matthew," Ada whispered, her eyes darting

around the crowd to ensure their conversation remained private. "I've noticed he's been distancing himself. Have you seen how he's been avoiding everyone lately?"

Wilma's eyes flickered with a mix of guilt and understanding. "I have noticed he's not on my porch." Wilma laughed.

"I know, but I'm not talking about that. Ever since Krystal started dating Jed, Matthew must feel like he's lost his place."

"I see what you mean. He always used to come over for a meal even when he wasn't invited. He was always welcome, though."

Ada sighed deeply as her fork hovered over the chicken. "Your home was a refuge for him, especially with him being away from his parents. He's just a boy at heart. Now, with Krystal's attention diverted, he feels he's lost both a friend and a safe place."

"I didn't realize he felt that way," Wilma admitted. "He just stopped coming to my house. Maybe I should've told him he was welcome, but then things might've become difficult for Krystal. Oh dear, there's no easy answer."

Matthew, standing off to the side with a distant look in his eyes, seemed oblivious to their conversation. Ada could see the signs of pain and rejection etched on his face.

"He's hurt, Wilma," Ada whispered.

Wilma's gaze settled on Matthew, feeling a pang of

guilt. "You're right, Ada. He needs to know we still care about him."

"He knows I do. It's you I'm thinking of. I mean, his relationship with you, seeing that he only lives next door to you. He felt he could come and go and now he can't."

"I don't know what to do or what to say."

Ada nodded, her eyes glistening with unshed tears. "Just say something before the rift becomes too wide to bridge."

Wilma took a deep breath. The joy and warmth of the gathering now seemed distant, overshadowed by the pain of a single soul. Determinedly, she rose from her seat, smoothing her apron and walking toward Matthew.

"Matthew?" Her voice wavered just a touch, betraying her anxiety.

He turned, surprise evident in his eyes. "Wilma?"

She approached him, her hands folded in front of her. "Can we talk for a moment?"

He hesitated but finally nodded. They moved to a quieter corner. The scent of fresh grass and blooming Spring flowers enveloped them, adding a touch of serenity to the intense atmosphere.

"I've noticed you've not been around my porch lately," Wilma began, trying to ease the seriousness.

Matthew's lips quirked in a small smile. "I thought it might be better that way. With Krystal and Jed... I felt things were different."

Wilma sighed, "Matthew, you've always been welcome at my home. I regret not making that clear when things began changing. I didn't want you to feel pushed out."

He looked away, swallowing hard. "It's not just about being welcome, Wilma. It's about belonging. When Krystal started dating Jed, I felt... replaced."

"I can see how things have become awkward," Wilma said gently touching his arm. "And as for my home, it has and always will be open to you. I should have told you that a while ago."

Matthew blinked rapidly, fighting the emotion threatening to spill. "I just miss the days when things were simpler, when I felt like I had a place that felt like home."

"You'll always have a place, Matthew. With Krystal, with me, and in this community. Relationships evolve, and sometimes we need to change with them. But that doesn't mean you're ever left out."

His voice was a mere whisper when he asked, "I've been worried about Krystal. Are they talking about marriage?"

Wilma was put on the spot. "I don't want to be accused of telling tales, but I believe things are strongly headed that way. That's all I'll say."

Matthew's shoulders slumped. "Well, at least I know. Thank you for talking with me, Wilma. And congratulations about Favor."

Wilma's eyebrows shot up. "How did you find out about that?"

"Don't worry. I won't tell." Matthew gave her a wink.

Wilma could only think that Jared might have said something. She only hoped that Favor didn't find out that the news of her pregnancy was spreading.

CHAPTER 31

The following Saturday, Wilma was again alone with Jared as they sat on the porch watching the orchard workers arriving and the odd truck getting filled with boxes of apples.

"You haven't forgotten about the birdhouse, have you?" Jared asked as they sat on the porch steps, enjoying the sunshine.

"Of course not." Wilma had hoped he'd forget because she had no idea how to begin such a task. "We'll find everything we need in Levi's old tool room."

"Can we do it now?"

"Yes."

She stood up and Jared dashed off ahead of her and ran into the barn which held the tool room.

When she got there, Jared was waiting patiently at the door of the room.

"Let's see what we can find," Wilma said as she

opened the door, revealing a room filled with memories and worn-out tools. The smell of aged wood shavings and metal filled their nostrils as they stepped inside.

"Look, here are some sheets of wood!" Jared exclaimed, pointing to a stack of weathered planks that lay against the wall. He picked one up, running his fingers along the rough surface, imagining the birds that would soon call it home.

"Perfect," Wilma agreed. Her thoughts wandered to how much she cherished family moments like these – simple acts of togetherness that brought her more comfort than any material possession ever could. Jared would look back and remember the moment he made this birdhouse with her. Well, she hoped that would happen. If not, he'd remember when they both had tried and failed to make a birdhouse.

"Aunt Wilma, do you think we have nails and a saw around here too?" Jared inquired.

"Ah, let me check Levi's old toolbox." She opened a rusty metal box that sat atop a wooden workbench. With a soft smile, she pulled out a handful of nails and a slightly rusted, yet still sharp, saw. "Here we go, Jared. This should be everything we need."

"Great, let's get started."

Wilma sniffed the air. "Why don't we do it outside in the fresh air? We'll go to the back of the house near where the wood is chopped."

"Okay, let's go."

CHAPTER 32

Wilma sat on an old chair and Jared kneeled next to her, a few wooden boards and tools spread out before them. The sun cast dappled patterns through the apple trees, and a warm breeze rustled the grasses in the nearby fields.

"Alright, Jared," Wilma said, her eyes twinkling as she held up one of the sheets of wood. "How do you imagine our birdhouse should look?"

Jared studied the wood for a moment before his face lit up with excitement. "I think it should have a sloping roof to keep the rain off and a little round hole for the birds to fly in."

"That sounds like a good idea." She carefully marked the wood with a pencil, preparing to make the first cut with the saw. Then with her tongue between her teeth and squinting at the line she'd drawn, she began sawing.

"Hello, Wilma!" a familiar voice called out, causing her to pause mid-cut.

"Ah, Eli. What brings you here today?"

"Thought I'd pay a visit and see how you're doing," he replied as he surveyed the scene before him. "What are you doing?"

"Building a birdhouse."

"Well, we're trying," Wilma confirmed, her gaze lingering on the saw in her hand. "Jared and I thought it would be a nice addition to the backyard. We can look out the kitchen window and see the visiting birds."

"Yeah," Jared agreed.

Eli leaned in closer to examine their work. "May I offer some suggestions?" he asked gently.

"Of course. We could use all the help we can get," Wilma said.

"First, when cutting the wood, try holding the saw at a slight angle," Eli demonstrated, adjusting Wilma's grip. "It helps with precision and control."

"Ah, I see," Wilma murmured, her brow furrowing in concentration as she attempted the new technique.

"Next, for the birdhouse's entrance, I recommend using a small drill hole before enlarging it," Eli continued, his voice steady and patient. "This helps prevent the wood from splitting."

"Thank you, Eli." Wilma glanced over at Jared, who was watching intently, his eyes wide with curiosity.

"Anytime, Wilma," Eli smiled, his eyes crinkling

warmly at the corners. "I'm always happy to lend a hand."

"What can I do?" Jared asked.

Eli crouched down to Jared's level, his friendly demeanor putting the boy at ease. "Well, young man, you can be in charge of painting once we've got this all assembled. How does that sound?"

Jared's eyes lit up. "I'd love that! Can we paint it blue? Birds like blue, right?"

Eli chuckled, "They might. Blue could remind them of the sky. But first, let's finish building it."

The day wore on, with the three of them working harmoniously together. Under Eli's guidance, they made good progress. The sounds of sawing, drilling, and light laughter added to all the other sounds of the busy orchard. The birdhouse began to take shape.

"Look at that!" Wilma said, admiring their handiwork. "With a bit of paint, it'll be perfect."

Jared grinned from ear to ear. "This is the best birdhouse ever!"

After a few hours, the trio looked at their finished project with satisfaction.

"Thank you, Eli," Wilma said sincerely, offering him a warm smile. "I don't think we could've done this without you."

"It was my pleasure," Eli replied, wiping his hands on a cloth. "Always happy to help, especially with such enthusiastic builders."

Jared wrapped his small arms around Eli's leg. "Thanks for teaching us, Eli."

Eli bent down, ruffling Jared's hair gently. "Anytime. Remember, every project is an adventure and an opportunity to learn how to do things better. Enjoy every step of the way."

"How about some lunch before we go looking for some paint?"

Eli grinned. "Sounds good to me."

"Do we have paint?" Jared asked.

"There's sure to be some in Levi's tool room."

The three of them walked into the house and Jared insisted on taking his birdhouse with him.

AFTER THEY ATE, they found some yellow paint in the shed and some red roof paint. Jared spent the next hour painstakingly painting the bird house, one small brush stroke at a time.

Wilma and Eli looked on as they drank tea and nibbled on sugar cookies.

"Finished," Jared yelled suddenly.

"Good work, Jared," Wilma called out.

Jared's eyes sparkled with delight as he gazed at the birdhouse, its carefully crafted roof and entrance gleaming in the sunlight. He jumped up and down unable to contain his joy. "It's perfect, Aunt Wilma! Just perfect. Now the birds will have somewhere to go when it rains."

"They will indeed," Eli added with a nod, his eyes softening as he watched the boy's enthusiasm. "You both did an excellent job."

"Thank you for all your help, Eli," Wilma murmured.

"Can we make more, Aunt Wilma?" Jared asked eagerly. "We could put them all around the orchard. We'll have the happiest birds. They'll all want to live here."

"I don't think Florence will want too many birds in the orchard. Or the wrong kinds of birds."

Jared's head tilted to one side. "What are the wrong birds?"

"Starlings. I believe they eat the apples from the inside out. I don't think we have those around here anymore. Let's focus on finding the perfect spot for this one first," she suggested gently, not wanting to dampen Jared's enthusiasm.

"Alright," Jared agreed. He looked at the birdhouse once more, his face a picture of determination. "But I'm going to make sure this is the best home any bird could ever wish for."

Wilma chuckled. "They'll love it. Let's find a spot in one of the regular trees close to the house and not in the orchard."

"You said we could watch them from the kitchen window."

"Yes."

As the three of them chose a spot, Wilma was thankful that Eli hadn't mentioned a word about his cousin, Obadiah.

"What about this tree?" Jared's voice brought her back to the present as he pointed to a sturdy oak standing tall beside their home. Its branches stretched out like welcoming arms, beckoning them closer.

"Perfect, Jared," Wilma agreed, smiling at the choice. "It's close enough to the house, yet far enough from the orchard."

"Alright, let's put it up. We'll have to be careful of the wet paint." Jared said.

"It should be dry soon. Anyway, just hold it by that metal loop. That's how you'll attach it to the tree. I'll get a ladder." Eli was gone for a couple of minutes and returned with a ladder.

As Wilma held the ladder steady, Jared carefully climbed up, his small hands gripping the rungs with determination. He reached the designated branch, secured the birdhouse, and climbed back down.

"Good job, Jared. You've made a wonderful home for our feathered friends," Eli said.

Jared grinned as he stared up at the tree. "I can't wait to see who moves in."

"Neither can I." Wilma put her arm around Jared's shoulders.

CHAPTER 33

*F*lorence sat at her writing desk, pen in hand, as she carefully crafted a letter to her stepsisters, Mercy and Honor. She wanted to ensure they wouldn't miss Debbie's wedding, and she hoped it would turn into a grand family reunion. With her newborn baby asleep, it was a rare moment of peace in the house.

As she wrote, she heard the front door open and the sound of giggling. Florence looked up to see Carter entering the house, carrying their young daughter Iris, who was covered in dirt from head to toe. Her curly hair was disheveled, and her face was smeared with mud.

"Carter, what on earth happened?" Florence exclaimed, trying not to laugh at the sight.

Carter grinned sheepishly. "Well, we were in the

garden, and she discovered a big pile of dirt. You know how curious she is. She couldn't resist playing in it."

Iris beamed proudly, showing off her dirt-covered hands.

"I can see that," Florence said, chuckling. "Well, I suppose it's time for a bath."

Carter nodded and headed toward the bathroom with Iris still in his arms. "I'll take care of this. What are you up to, anyway?"

Florence returned to her letter with a smile. "I'm writing to Mercy and Honor. I want to make sure they'll be at Debbie's wedding. And I'm hoping to turn it into a family reunion of sorts."

Carter raised an eyebrow, intrigued. "A family reunion? You want everyone to be there?"

"Yes, exactly!" Florence said, her eyes lighting up with excitement. "I want Mercy and Honor to come with their families, of course, and also Earl and Miriam with all their children. It's been too long since we've all been together."

Carter nodded in agreement. "I think that's a great idea. It'll mean so much to Debbie to have everyone there."

"I think so too. She's cut communication with her parents and Jared's grandparents from the other side," Florence said.

Carter left the room with Iris while Florence started a letter to Earl.

As she finished and sealed that letter, Carter walked

back into the room, now with a clean and giggling Iris. "All cleaned up and ready for some more mischief," he said with a playful grin.

Florence laughed and reached out to tickle Iris, who squealed with delight. Then Iris headed for the door.

"Hey, where are you going?" Carter asked.

"To play with Spot."

Carter shook his head. "No more dirt, okay?"

"I'm not doing that. I'm only going to play with Spot." With that, Iris headed out the door.

Carter stood by Florence's side and looked down at the letter that were stamped and ready to go. "So, you only write one letter to both sisters?"

"I addressed it to Mercy but the letter is to Honor as well."

"I see. We've saved money on a stamp."

Florence laughed. "I guess there is that advantage as well. The two of them are close, so they can read it together. Oh, I do hope they come."

"You're really looking forward to this wedding, aren't you?"

"I am."

"With you in charge, it will be a great wedding."

Florence laughed. "I'm not in charge of anything. All I'm doing is making the dresses."

Carter raised an eyebrow playfully. "Just making the dresses? You're the one with the vision, Florence. You could make this wedding extra special."

"Well, I just want it to be a special day for Debbie,

and having everyone there would make it even more meaningful."

Carter pulled Florence to her feet and then wrapped his arms around her. "You have a way of bringing people together, you know? And I have no doubt that Debbie's wedding will be beautiful."

"I hope so," Florence said, resting her head on his shoulder. "I just want her to be happy. She's been through so much, and she deserves all the happiness in the world."

"She does, and she's lucky to have you as a friend," Carter said, planting a soft kiss on her forehead.

Florence smiled, feeling a sense of warmth and contentment. "I'm lucky to have her too."

Iris rushed back into the house, cheeks flushed with excitement. "Dad, Spot wants to play catch! Can we, please? I won't get dirty again, it's just catch."

Carter chuckled. "Sure thing, I'll help. Let's play catch."

Florence returned to her writing desk, thinking about Mercy and Honor. She knew there had been some past conflicts and misunderstandings, but she hoped this wedding would be an opportunity for healing and reconciliation.

Besides, most families had their disagreements. Not everyone got along all the time and the Baker/Bruner family was no different.

Staring at the letters, Florence knew their replies would determine whether her dream of a family reunion would come true, but she remained optimistic. She grabbed the letters, stood up, and then popped the letters into her nearby handbag to post the next day.

As she joined Carter and Iris outside to play catch with Spot, she couldn't help but feel grateful for her family and the love that surrounded her. With Wilma slowly accepting Carter into her life, Carter was more content too.

CHAPTER 34

$\mathcal{T}$he next morning, Wilma was at the small shop on her orchard with Ada, arranging the store ready for customers.

She dusted a row of glass jars filled with homemade preserves while Ada was busy with candy apples, wrapping each one individually and then securing the clear wrapping with a red ribbon.

"The place looks good, Wilma. I think we'll have a good day. More and more people are coming now that word has gotten out that we've opened the shop this year."

Wilma agreed. "It's certainly been productive so far."

Just as Wilma spoke those words, the door to the shop creaked open and a cold draft blew in, causing the women to shiver.

In strode the horrible man who had taken Red. His

dirty boots left muddy footprints on the wooden floor, and his unkempt beard framed a menacing scowl.

"Ah, there you are, Mrs. Baker," he sneered, his voice like gravel. "I heard you've been asking around about my dog. Have you found it?"

Wilma's heart raced, her hands trembling slightly as she gripped the edge of the counter for support. She didn't bother to correct him and tell him that she was now Mrs. Bruner. Instead, she exchanged a brief, concerned glance with Ada before responding. "No, I haven't found your dog. We've been too busy with our work here at the shop."

"Is that so?" The man's dark eyes narrowed suspiciously, his gaze darting between the two women. "Well, if you do find it, make sure you let me know. It's not some stray you can just take in and call your own. It's mine by law."

Wilma nodded, her voice barely above a whisper. "If we see him, we'll let you know right away."

For a moment, the man seemed appeased by Wilma's response, but then he cast one last lingering, distrustful look at both women before turning on his heel and stomping out of the shop.

As the door slammed shut behind him, Wilma let out a shaky breath, her heart pounding in her chest. She turned to Ada, who had been standing silently by her side throughout the encounter. "Oh, Ada... I don't know what I would have done if you weren't here with me."

Ada reached over to grasp Wilma's hand. "We'll make a rule that no one is alone in the shop, okay?"

Wilma nodded. Then she moved to the window and looked out to make sure the man had gone.

She watched the man's retreating figure, her heart pounding like a thousand galloping horses. She knew he didn't believe her, and she feared he'd come back at some point if Red stayed missing.

"Wilma, don't worry. He's gone now."

But before Wilma could reply, the man suddenly stopped in his tracks and turned around, his eyes locked onto the house at the end of the driveway. With a determined stride, he began walking toward it, calling out, "Fred! Fred, come here, boy!"

Wilma's breath caught in her throat, and without a moment's hesitation, she burst out the door, her dress swishing urgently as she hurried to catch up with him. "Wait!"

The man paused and looked back at her, an eyebrow raised.

"He's not here. I told you that. Please leave." Then Wilma thought she saw something dangerous flicker behind his eyes. He ignored her and continued toward the house, still calling for the dog.

Wilma looked around for help. There had been so many orchard workers milling about this morning, but now there was no one to be seen.

To Wilma's horror, he marched right up to the house. As he stepped onto her porch, his boots scuffed against the worn wooden boards, each thud rattling through Wilma's chest. Wilma was right behind him to see what he would do.

The man's whistle pierced the air, sending a shiver down Wilma's spine. "Fred!" he called again, his voice gruff and impatient.

"Please," she implored, her heart pounding in her ears. "You must leave our property."

The man snorted, his lip curling into a sneer. "Did you think you could hide him? Maybe he's in the house."

"He's not in there. I don't have the dog. I already told you that."

He reached out, his hand hovering over the door handle, fingers twitching with anticipation.

Before Wilma could protest, the door opened from the inside. Eli, with a stern and protective look on his face, stood in the doorway, blocking the man's path.

"Can I help you?" Eli's voice was cold and measured, not at all friendly.

The man stopped, taken aback by Eli's unexpected appearance. "I'm here for my dog, Fred. This woman here says she doesn't have him, but I think she's lying."

Eli stepped forward, causing the man to take a step back. "I've been here a while, and I haven't seen any dog. I suggest you look elsewhere."

The man's bravado wavered, but he attempted to maintain his arrogant facade. He laughed. "Are you threatening me, old man?"

Eli's gaze was steady. "Just offering some friendly advice. You've already bothered this good woman enough for one day. As she said, there is no dog here."

The man's eyes darted between Wilma and Eli. "This ain't over," he muttered, though there was notably less conviction in his voice. Then he eyed Matthew's belongings on the porch. "I'll take this in exchange for the dog." He leaned over and scooped up Matthew's belongings which included Matthew's tiny camping stove.

"Those things are..." Wilma didn't want to make him mad so she stopped mid-sentence.

"Yeah. They're mine now." Narrowing his eyes, the man glared at Wilma with a venomous expression. With one last huff of frustration, he stormed back to his dusty pickup truck. He placed the items in the back and then got into the driver's seat, slamming the car door.

Eli watched him intently, ensuring he retreated from the property. Only when he was certain the man was gone did he turn his attention back to Wilma. "Are you okay?" he asked gently.

Wilma, shaken by the confrontation, nodded, trying to steady her breathing. "Yes, thank you, Eli. I don't know what he would have done if you hadn't been there. He was going into my house."

Eli's eyes softened. "I told you, Wilma, friends look out for one another. You can count on that."

She managed a small smile. "I'm starting to see that, Eli. Thank you again."

Ada, having witnessed the exchange from the shop, rushed over, wrapping an arm around Wilma for support. "That was too close," she whispered.

"Yes, but we're safe now," Wilma replied, smiling at Eli.

"What was he carrying?" Ada asked.

"He took all of Matthew's things. He said it was payment for the dog. He thought the dog was here somewhere."

Ada chuckled. "Serves Matthew right for leaving those things there for so long."

Wilma sighed. "I don't know what to tell Matthew."

"I'll tell him. You have enough to worry about." Ada turned her attention to Eli. "What were you doing in the house, Eli? I didn't even know you were here. Did you, Wilma?"

Wilma shook her head. "No."

Eli chuckled. "I came to fix this creaky door. No one was home when I knocked, so I let myself in."

"I totally forgot to ask someone to fix that door," Wilma said.

"No matter. I noticed it was creaky the other day when I was here. I was in the middle of oiling the hinges when I heard a whistle. I came out to see what was going on."

"It's a good thing you were here, Eli, just when Wilma needed you the most."

Eli chuckled. "Well, I've finished it." Eli demonstrated that the creak was gone by swinging the door open and closed a couple of times.

"Thank you, Eli. You must come for the evening meal tonight," Wilma insisted.

Eli gave a nod. "I'd like that."

CHAPTER 35

*B*ack at the shop that same afternoon, Wilma's fingers traced the edge of the rough wooden counter, her mind far from the apple goods shop.

She had to accept that Red was gone, but she was certain that man would not be back.

"Ada," she began hesitantly, "do you think I should be worried about not having a man around the house?"

Ada looked up from organizing Debbie's boxes of tea. "Why do you ask?"

"Today just brought it all back, you know? How vulnerable I felt when that man was here." Wilma swallowed hard, hating how her voice trembled. "I can't help but think that if I had someone... well, maybe things would be different. I wouldn't have been able to stop him going into the house."

"You're hardly ever alone. I'm here mostly every day and then there are Krystal and Debbie. Plus all the orchard workers coming and going. When it's not harvest time, there are a ton of people around."

"Thank you, Ada," Wilma whispered, letting herself find comfort in her friend's words. "I suppose I just need to remind myself of that more often."

"Exactly." Ada smiled warmly and returned to what she'd been doing.

As they continued their tasks, Wilma couldn't shake the lingering feeling of unease. The incident with the man had stirred up something deep within her, a vulnerability that being without a husband caused. "If I married again, then I wouldn't feel like this."

"Who would you marry? Obadiah?" Ada left the tea and walked over to Wilma. "He lives far away, and you were unsure about him which made me unsure. If you truly loved him, you wouldn't have let him go."

"I feel I did love him, but…"

"But what?" Ada asked.

"Marriages can work without love. But with him, there was love. I think that maybe I shouldn't have let him go."

Ada shook her head. "I don't know what to say to you. You had your reasons for the decision you made."

"I did, but now I don't know."

"Well, if you don't know, Wilma, how do you expect me to know? Just don't rush into anything. Okay?"

Wilma nodded and wished she could talk things

over with someone who understood. Ada had been married to only one man so how could she possibly understand?

Over the next couple of hours the shop bustled with customers coming in to purchase their favorite apple goods. Ada and Wilma worked together, their hands moving with practiced ease as they tended to the shop's needs.

Once they were alone again, Ada started tidying again.

"Wilma, look at this beautiful display of apple butter jars!" Ada exclaimed, breaking Wilma from her thoughts.

Smiling, Wilma joined Ada in admiring the neatly arranged jars. "They do look lovely. We've done well this season," she replied, trying to focus on the present moment.

Wilma's mind, however, kept drifting back to the man who had visited earlier that day.

"Do you think he'll come back?" Ada asked, seemingly sensing Wilma's thoughts.

Wilma sighed, her fingers unconsciously tracing the edge of a jar. "I hope not. I can't bear the thought of someone like him causing trouble here," she admitted.

Ada placed a comforting hand on Wilma's shoulder. "Don't worry. We'll keep an eye out for any suspicious characters. And remember, we have the community to support us. We're not alone in this."

"I know, Ada," Wilma replied, offering a faint smile. "I'm just feeling a bit rattled, that's all."

Ada nodded in understanding. "Everything will be fine."

The vulnerability Wilma had felt earlier in the day began to ebb away.

CHAPTER 36

It was mid-afternoon when Favor stood at the window of her kitchen, lost in thought as she watched the bishop approach on foot. She realized he probably had left his horse and buggy at Zeke's place and continued from there.

"Simon," she called out, her voice gently piercing the serene environment. "The bishop is here."

Her husband, Simon, appeared in the doorway. He nodded solemnly, readying himself for the bishop's message.

Together, they stepped outside. The bishop smiled warmly, extending a hand to both Simon and Favor.

"Good evening," he said. "I hope I'm not intruding."

"Of course not," replied Simon, "What brings you here today?"

"We've come to discuss a matter of housing," the bishop began. "Word has it that a ready-made house can be bought and transported to your parents' new land. It's old, but sturdy."

Melvin and Harriet, seated comfortably inside, overheard the conversation and joined them. "An interesting idea," Melvin mused. "However, I believe we must consider all options carefully."

Favor's fingers played with the hem of her apron. "Simon," she began, "I have a thought."

Simon looked at her, curiosity filling his eyes. "What is it?"

"Why don't we build onto our house here, creating a bigger house for us all, but divide it into two? Harriet and Melvin can be close, but we'll all have our independence."

Everyone was silent contemplating Favor's suggestion. Melvin was the first to speak. "Are you sure that's what you want, Favor?"

Simon frowned at Favor. "Maybe we should talk in private before we make any huge decisions."

Favor had seen the value of having Simon's parents around. Melvin was no trouble, and Harriet had been a lot less bossy and a whole lot more willing to help. Once the baby arrived, Favor knew she'd need Harriet even more. "Well, what do you think?" Favor asked her husband.

"I'm fine with it, but have you thought this through?"

Favor nodded. "I see it's the solution. As Pa said the

other day, if we do something like that, it'll leave more farmland free for grazing and for yards and pens."

The bishop nodded in agreement.

"We'd love that as long as you're sure you won't change your mind, Favor," Harriet said.

"I won't change my mind."

"Then it's settled," Simon said, relief evident in his voice. "We'll start planning the addition soon."

Melvin patted Simon's shoulder, "Family is everything. Ma and I are delighted."

FAVOR DROVE over to Cherish's house to share the latest news with her. Of course, that was against Harriet's approval. If it were up to Harriet, Favor wouldn't leave the house until after the baby was born. In the end, Favor had gotten her way.

Favor and Cherish sat in Cherish's living room. "So, you seem distracted. What's wrong?"

Favor laughed. "Oh, Cherish, you sound like *Mamm*. That's what she always says when I call her."

"It's just I'm surprised to see you here after you've been so sick."

"I'm fine." Favor took a deep breath, "I need to talk to you about something." She looked into Cherish's eyes, her expression serious.

Cherish set aside the knitting she had been working

on and gave Favor her full attention. "Of course, what is it?" she asked.

"I've been thinking about Harriet and Melvin," Favor said, choosing her words carefully. "And I've come to a decision." She hesitated for a moment before continuing. "Simon and I offered them... well, we said they could build an adjoining dwelling onto our house."

Cherish's eyes widened in surprise, her heart pounding with shock. "What?" she exclaimed, her voice slightly louder than she intended. "Favor, that's far too close. Don't you remember how you were trying to escape from them?"

"I know, but—"

Cherish sprang to her feet and started pacing. "Don't they know they can buy the land next to you? They said they were going to buy it and they were allowed to."

"They are buying it, but we want to keep more of the land free for the alpacas."

Cherish sat down again. "Alpacas," she echoed. "But don't you remember why you wanted to come here in the first place? You wanted to get away from them so you and Simon could be by yourselves."

"I remember, Cherish. But things are different now. Harriet has changed, and she's been so helpful to us. She's been like a second mother to me. She looked after me when I was sick, and I believe she'll continue to be a great help when the baby arrives."

Cherish sighed, her anxiety still evident. "I know she's been helpful, but living right next door? It's too close, Favor. You said an adjoining house? That's worse. Don't do it."

Favor reached out and took Cherish's hand in hers. "I understand your reservations, but think about it," she said softly. "With Harriet and Melvin living nearby, we'll have the support of family just a few steps away. It'll be easier, and Harriet can watch the baby when I need a break. I do agree that in the past Simon and I wanted to be alone, but now we have someone else to think about." Favor put a hand over her belly.

Cherish chewed on her bottom lip, remembering how upset Favor had been with Harriet in the past. "I was only joking when I said Harriet would be a good help to you. I mean she will, but that doesn't mean she needs to live so close."

"I believe people can change, and Harriet has shown that she's willing to change for the better."

Cherish sighed. "I find it just weird how you can do a complete turnaround. You escaped and then they followed within days."

"I know, but she is really respecting that the house is mine."

Cherish shook her head. "Is she? I don't think so. She's taken over your house from the moment she stepped a foot in the door. You just can't see it."

Favor laughed. "Don't be so serious. It's fine, really. I appreciate that you care about my feelings."

"I always will do that. Maybe the pregnancy has clouded your judgment somehow. I know. Why don't you wait until after the baby is born before you make the decision?"

"It's too late. Melvin is already drawing up plans."

Cherish's mouth fell open in horror.

"Just relax. I have everything under control. It's all working out fine and I owe you and Malachi a big thank you."

"We're happy to do whatever we can. Can I get you something to eat?"

"No. I'm still not very hungry. Unless, do you have chocolate?"

"I sure do." As Cherish headed to the kitchen to fetch some chocolate, she couldn't help but worry. Harriet and Melvin living so close to Favor was a bad idea. She saw trouble ahead.

The biggest issue was, why couldn't Favor see it?

CHAPTER 37

When Wilma and Ada closed up the shop for the day, they headed to the house discussing what they'd make for dinner.

First, Wilma took Ada around the back of the house and showed her Jared's birdhouse. "Isn't it beautiful, Ada? Eli helped Jared and me make it."

Ada could see how straight the edges were and the roof was sloped at a pleasing angle. It looked professionally made. "Very good. I'm guessing Eli did most of the work, *jah?*" Just then, they heard a rustling in the bushes nearby. Ada's eyes widened. "What was that?"

Wilma squinted in the direction of the noise, straining to see through the dense foliage. Suddenly, she spotted something emerging from the undergrowth.

"Red!" Wilma cried out, rushing over to hug the shaggy canine. He wagged his tail weakly, happy to see her despite his obvious pain. As she kneeled beside him, Wilma noticed how thin he was, his ribs nearly visible beneath his matted fur. His paws were bleeding, leaving small crimson stains on the grass.

"Get him inside, Wilma," Ada urged, her voice trembling. "Look at the poor thing."

Wilma nodded firmly, determination setting her jaw as she scooped Red up in her arms. For a large dog, he was light. "I don't know who you belong to, Red, but I won't let them hurt you again," she vowed softly.

The screen door creaked open, and she stepped into the kitchen, Ada following closely behind.

"Set him down on this blanket," Ada suggested as she folded it neatly on the floor.

"Jah, that's a good idea." Wilma carefully placed Red down. She met his trusting eyes and whispered, "I won't let that horrible man get his hands on you again, Red. I won't."

"Wilma," Ada hesitated before speaking, her voice wavering slightly, "that's dog stealing. That man's the rightful owner however fearful he may be."

"Ada, look at him." Wilma gestured to Red, his frail body shivering with pain. "He was starving and hurt when he came to me. No loving owner would allow this to happen. I've seen how he treats Red." Wilma hurried to get him food while Ada filled a dish with water and placed it down for him.

"Your heart is in the right place, Wilma, but we must follow the rules."

"I can't allow the dog to go with that man." Wilma's voice trembled with emotion. "Red deserves better. I can provide that for him."

Ada sighed, her eyes filled with understanding. "Just make sure you're not inviting trouble."

"Wait a moment. You heard him. He took Matthew's things as payment. So, that makes me the new owner."

"That's right. It does." Ada grinned.

Wilma pulled out a plate of roast leftovers from the previous night, the tender meat still fragrant and enticing. "He'll surely appreciate this. Red is a gift from *Gott*, sent to remind me that love can find us in unexpected ways."

"Love has a funny way of doing that, doesn't it?" Ada smiled softly, resting her hand on Wilma's shoulder.

"*Jah*, it does. Can you see what Red went through to come back to me?"

Ada looked at the dog and nodded.

"It seems Red and I belong together. We need each other."

"And what if the man comes back to get him?"

"I won't let him take Red. I'll simply remind him of what he said when he took that bundle of things off my porch."

Ada looked to say more, but she glanced down at Red's pitiful form and bit her lip, unable to argue further.

Wilma gave a nod, acknowledging her friend's unspoken agreement. Once he was finished eating, Wilma leaned down and patted him.

"Wilma, he still must be starving," Ada said quietly, casting a worried glance at Red. "Do you have any more food for him?"

"I agree that he could probably eat more, but if he hasn't eaten for days, I don't want to give him too much at once. What I gave him was a meal in itself. I'll give him more in a few hours."

"I hate to bring it up again, but are you certain about this? You have never been a dog lover."

"Red isn't just any dog," Wilma answered softly, her gaze never leaving Red. "He needs me, Ada." She hesitated for a moment, then added quietly, "And if I'm being honest, I think I need him too. He gives me something to care about every day."

Ada sighed, and though she still seemed doubtful, she nodded in understanding. "Well, then," she said, offering a small smile. "I suppose we have a new member of our family."

"*Jah,*" Wilma agreed, her eyes shining with love and gratitude as she watched Red closing his eyes to rest. The sight warmed her heart, and she leaned against the wall, feeling a sense of peace wash over her. "He came back to me, Ada," Wilma said softly, her voice reflecting the love she felt for this beaten but resilient dog.

"He knows where he's wanted," Ada replied.

As they stood together in the small kitchen, Wilma

couldn't help but think that this was what truly mattered in life. The connections made, the love given and received, and the determination to stand up for what was right— these were the true blessings bestowed upon them by God.

Wilma gently leaned down and stroked Red's head. "I'll take him to the vet tomorrow and get him checked over."

"I'm sure he'll be okay with some food in his belly, but you do that if you want," Ada replied.

"I feel I've got a lot in common with the dog somehow."

"Really? How so?"

"Like Red, I've faced some hardships in my life. The loss of my husbands, giving up a child, the struggles some years to keep the orchard running... and yet, here I am, still standing, still carrying on."

"True," Ada agreed, nodding thoughtfully. "You've always been resilient, Wilma. But what does that have to do with Red?"

"Perhaps it's our shared determination to survive, no matter the odds," Wilma mused, watching as Red's chest rose and fell in a steady rhythm. "Or maybe it's the simple fact that we both need someone to care for us, and to love us unconditionally."

"Wilma, you know you're loved," Ada assured her.

"Thank you, Ada," Wilma said. "I just can't help but feel a connection with Red. I mean, he just appeared here... like he found me."

"We'll never know the mind of *Gott*. He sets everything in its place."

As they continued to talk, Wilma felt a sense of peace surrounding her.

She knew that she and Red had both faced their share of challenges, but together, it was clear that they had found their place in the world.

And for now, that was enough.

Thank you for reading Amish Harvest Time.

www.SamanthaPriceAuthor.com

For a downloadable series reading order of all Samantha Price's books, scan below.

THE NEXT BOOK IN THE AMISH BONNET SISTERS

The next book in The Amish Bonnet Sisters series is: Book 39 Whispers of Change.

All the Baker girls are home to help with Debbie's wedding. But the reunion isn't just about the wedding preparations. Old memories resurface, unresolved feelings stir, and the tight-knit bond of the Baker sisters is tested as never before.

Will the promise of Debbie's wedding day bring them closer or unveil divides that have long been hidden?

ABOUT SAMANTHA PRICE

Samantha Price is a USA Today bestselling and Kindle All Stars author of Amish romance books and cozy mysteries. She was raised Brethren and has a deep affinity for the Amish way of life, which she has explored extensively with over a decade of research. She is mother to two pampered rescue cats, and a very spoiled staffy with separation issues.

www.SamanthaPriceAuthor.com

Made in the USA
Middletown, DE
17 March 2024